Flying

THE COAST SKYWAYS

or Jack Ralston's
Swift Patrol

Flying

THE COAST SKYWAYS

or Jack Ralston's
Swift Patrol

WILDSIDE PRESS

CONTENTS

By Ambrose Newcomb

INTRODUCTION

The "Sky Detectives" series, written by Ambrose Newcomb, consists of 6 books, all published between 1930 and 1931 by the Goldsmith Publishing Company:

The Sky Detectives; or, How Jack Ralston Got his Man
Eagles of the Sky; or, With Jack Ralston along the Air Lanes
Wings Over the Rockies; or, Jack Ralston's New Cloud Chaser
The Sky Pilot's Great Chase; or, Jack Ralston's Dead Stick Landing
Trackers of the Fog Pack; or, Jack Ralston Flying Blind
Flying the Coast Skyways; or, Jack Ralston's Swift Patrol

They are typical of the adventure series aimed at boys of the era, which often relied on new inventions as a theme. We had the "Motion Picture Chums," the "Moving Picture Comrades," and the "Moving Picture Boys" when cinemas first opened; the "Radio Boys" when radio was introduced, and the "Slim Tyler Air Stories" (also launched in 1930) and the "Sky Flyers" (also 1931), among many others. You can chart the interests of children of the era by the series titles.

In this case, the Goldsmith Company went for a trifecta of themes: mysteries, aviation, and patriotism. The series featured Jack Ralston and his pal "Perk," a pair of famous air pilots, who help the U.S. government unravel problems that baffle even the Secret Service. Each book told a complete story.

I suspect "Ambrose Newcomb" of being the pseudonym for several different authors. Goldsmith was a notoriously low-end publisher, printing with the cheapest possible paper and reusing the same cover art on all books in a series. It's a wonder kids could keep the stories straight. They sold their books at bargain prices in department stores, as well as to libraries.

Despite that, the author—or authors—behind "Ambrose Newcomb" did a good job, with well-plotted stories filled with action. They delighted their audience . . . but not enough to continue beyond the initial 6 volumes in the series. (Edward Stratemeyer, the creative force behind the Stratemeyer Syndicate, which was the most successful children's book packager of the period, always launched a new series with a half dozen books as a way to gauge interest. Other publishers followed his example.)

Enjoy this trip to the early days of air travel, when the Great War was long over, World War II was still in the future, and citizens felt free to take to the skies.

—John Betancourt
Cabin John, Maryland

Flying

THE COAST SKYWAYS

or Jack Ralston's Swift Patrol

FLYING THE COAST SKYWAYS

CHAPTER I

By Airline to Atlanta

"Big smoke dead ahead, partner!"

"I've been expecting to hear you announce that fact, Per—I mean Wally!"

"Kinder guess naow it mout be Birmingham, eh, what, Boss?"

"No other—you hit the nail on the head that time, Mr. Observer."

"Huh! my *native* town, which I'm naow agwine to see fur the fust time."

"Better get out of the habit of making such crazy cracks, brother—what if any one overheard you, and took a notion in his head you might be somebody other than just a Down-in-Dixie product from Alabama,—raised in the North, where you acquired a whiff of the dialect of a Canuck —and by name Wallace J. Corkendell, though generally answering to plain *Wally*."

"Hot-diggetty-dig! that ere smoke cloud sure looks jest like an ole peasoup fog-pack we done got lost in not so far back. By gravy! I doant b'lieve we'll even git one squint at the pesky city as we fly over the same!"

"I can easily see where I'm bound to have a lot of fun listening to you trying to talk in three different lingoes, all mixed up in one great mess—Yankee, your native brogue; Canadian patios, contracted while with the Northwest Mounted Police; and now a pidgin English, such as a Southern colored boy might use. I only hope such a mixture doesn't queer the big game we've got laid out ahead for us, whatever its nature proves to be."

"I er-*reckons—yeou* says I gotter use that word right along naow, 'cause no Alabama white or black boy never does *guess* anything—I reckons, suh, I'll git a strangle-holt on the way a gen-u-ine cracker keeps up his end o' a talkie—given a little time fo' practice."

"That begins to sound like the real stuff, comrade," observed Jack; and despite the clamor of engine exhaust, and whirling propellers both of them were able to hear every word uttered, simply because they were wearing their usual earphone attachments, without which they never made a flight. "I'm beginning to feel encouraged to believe you'll come through with flying colors. There, we're directly over Birmingham, and going strong to eastward."

"Huh! I'm right glad yeou done tole me so, suh," Perk hastened to reply, doubtless with one of his usual chuckles; "'case all I kin make aout's a black

smudge o' smoke ahuggin' the ground, with a few
church steeples apokin' a finger through the same.
So, there she lies, my own, my native city! Ain't it
affectin', though, ole pal, acomin' back like this,
after many years, an' discoverin' that same thick
smoke fog asettled daown on the dear old place?
Gee whiz! I'm jest awcnderin' whether us Southern kids ever *did* have a gen-u-ine ole swimmin'-
hole in them *won*-derful days, eh, what?"

When they were positively alone, and no danger
of crafty eavesdroppers picking up their words,
the two cronies were pleased to extract a certain
amount of fun out of their assumed characters—
for Jack Ralston of course was also sailing under
a *nom-de-guerre*, as well as his best pal—with
him the new name was "Rodman Warrington,"
and he was supposed to be a rich and eccentric New
York City sportsman, weary of the routine of the
Carrituck Sound shcoting club to which he belonged, and ardently desirous of exploring the
various bays, sounds and twisting rivers along the
wild coast of North and South Carolina, as well as
Georgia.

"To be sure they did, brother," Jack was saying,
reassuringly, in reply to the skeptical question
propounded by his running mate; "if you stop
and think you'll remember how every American
boy who grew up and amounted to shucks was

always getting a great thrill out of memories of such a meeting-place, where all the boys took occasion to show off in doing stunts with a diving board."

"Say, naow 'at we've left dear ole Birmingham in the rear, haow long 'fore we drop daown on Candler Field outside Atlanta?"

"Depends on what time we keep making," Jack informed him; "we're speeding along at a hundred-and-twenty clip just now, with only two motors working; and if there was any necessity for fetching it up to an even hundred-and-fifty we could easily enough do the same—and then some. I reckon we'll come in sight of Candler Field in about an hour-and-a-half—the chart tells me it's something like one-fifty miles, as the bee flies, between this Southern Pittsburgh and the Capital of Georgia."

"Meanin' to stop over in Atlanta long, partner?" demanded Perk; who apparently was not wholly advised of his leader's plans, as far as they were matured, and as usual "wanted to know."

"Around twenty-four hours, possibly less, buddy," Jack explained. "We've an appointment, made for us from Headquarters in Washington, to meet up with a certain official connected with the Secret Service, who holds forth in Atlanta —from him we'll receive a certain amount of information, and be referred to another party, high in the secrets of the Service in Charleston. When we jump off from that South Carolina city we'll know all we're expected to carry out—what we've been called east to accomplish. There, that's everything in a nutshell; I'm as much in the dark as you, even though I reckon I've figured things out, if a bit hazily, to tell the truth."

"We're goin' after some sort o' big game, I er-reckon, partner?" Perk speculated, his manner making the remark seem like a question.

"No doubt about that, boy—they wouldn't have called for us to fly all the way from San Diego, (with two necessary stops to prevent spies from learning as to who we are, and why we're heading east) if it hadn't been that some others in the Secret Service had played their innings—and fallen asleep at the switch."

"Hot-diggetty-dig! I'd say that'd be a neat compliment they're givin' us, ole hoss," Perk exulted; as enthusiastic as a boy over a Christmas present of a brand new shiny pair of club skates. "Another thing I'd like to hear tell 'baout, Ja—er, Mr. Warrin'ton, suh."

"As what, partner—you'll notice that I'm trying to call you all sorts of chummy names—that's for the purpose of trying to forget I ever knew you as Perk, or Gabe Perkiser. If you do the same there'll be less chance of giving our game away; for if any kind of quick-witted spies should hear us exchanging words they'd remember the real names of the two sky detectives who were playing particular hob with gents who gave Uncle Sammy the laugh. Now, I reckon you're referring to that letter I had just before we lifted out ship at San Diego last night."

"Yeou said it, er-ole pal," replied Perk, catching his treacherous tongue just in the nick of time. "I kinder—reckoned it mout acome from the gent over in San Diego, who's been aour boss since we started operations 'long the Coast."

"A fair enough guess, brother," Jack told him; "because that's the official who gave us the order to break away, and what to do on the skyway east. There was also some interesting information concerning the job we finished up some weeks back; and I meant to hand that over to you; but somehow failed to connect."

"I'm right tickled to hear that, suh—fack is I'd begun to feel they wasn't zactly treatin' us white, not sayin' as haow we'd done the Service proud, the way we fetched Slim Garrabrant back after he'd broke loose from the pen, an' started his ole tricks again."*

"Oh! they were quite enthusiastic about the success of our work, after others had fallen down

*See "Trackers of the Fog Pack."

on the job—that is, as warm as those cold people at Headquarters ever do get, it being against their principles to over praise those working under them, for fear of giving the poor guys the big-head. You can read the letter before I destroy it, brother. The Big Boss in L. A. also wrote that Slippery Slim had been safely returned to his former cell in Leavenworth, and with an added sentence; so, as they'll watch him closer from now on, there's small chance of our ever running up against him after this."

"Well, he was a good guy when it came to tacklin' big games, I'll tell the whole world," observed the satisfied Perk; who again busied himself with his reliable binoculars, eagerly surveying the checkered landscape a mile or more under the bottom of their fuselage; and which continued to prove of considerable interest to Perk, this being actually the first time he had ever passed over that section of the Southland, despite his absurd claim to having spent his boyhood days in Birmingham, Ala.

The time drifted along, with their speed undiminished. Pine woods, tracts of corn, cotton, tobacco; acres of fruit trees, pecan groves, even sugarcane patches—all these signs of the Southland he kept seeing as the miles flew past.

"I kinder—er-reckons as haow we've done shot

past the dividin' line 'tween Alabam 'nd Georgia, boss," he presently announced, with a grand air of superior knowledge; "case I jest seen a town squatted on a river, an' painted on the roof o' a house was a name, fo' the benefit o' fliers like weuns—Tallapoosa she read, which tells me that must a been the river Tallapoosa—all bein' 'cross the line in Harlson County, Georgia, ('cordin' to my map here.) If that's correct we right naow ain't more'n fifty miles from aour goal—less'n half an hour yet to fly."

"You are hot on the trail, comrade," Jack assured him. "Keep your eyes skinned to pick up another smoke cloud dead ahead, which will be the first sign of our nearing Atlanta, the New York City of the South."

Perk continued to watch and wait, until finally he gave a half suppressed whoop, to add exultantly:

"It's a *big* smoke smudge, all right, buddy; so we're rushing daown on aour goal like a river afire; which pleases a feller called Wally okay, yeou bet!"

CHAPTER II

The Cipher Letter

Jack did not seem to be at all surprised when his best pal made this abrupt announcement; but then he always kept himself prepared for coming events.

"I was expecting to hear you say that, buddy;" he told his mate; "for the past fifty miles on, our string up to date had about run through. I reckon we'll be on foot before many more minutes. Get the airport yet—Wally?"

"Sure do, and right naow I kin glimpse a big—looks like our Fokker, agoin' to drop daown."

"Yes, possibly belongs to either of the latest lines using Candler Field for a base—Eastern Air Transport, for passengers and mail; and Southern Air Fast Express—covering the route between Los Angeles and Atlanta—both now-a-days carrying capacity loads, the papers have been saying."

"Shucks! takes yeou to git things daown pat, Big Boss," Perk went on to comment. "Where do we go from here, Mister?"

"After we've made arrangements for housing our crate," explained Jack, good-naturedly—although he had told his chum the same thing at least twice before the present occasion—Perk could be so forgetful, he remembered—"we'll make straight for the Henry Grady Hotel, where we'll find a letter in code awaiting us, unless there's been a nasty hitch in the arrangements."

"But—yeou said we had to meet up with some gent here, partner?"

"That's right, too, Wally; but only after I've decoded the letter from Headquarters, which is going to put us wise about the nature of our present big adventure. No great hurry to get moving on, as far as I know at present; so it might be we can hang around Atlanta a day or more. But both of us will have to play our parts, and fend off any too inquisitive newspaper men. I've learned that the Atlanta reporters are keen on picking up every scrap of aviation news possible, so's to make up a story that will go well. We shun that sort of notoriety, don't forget, brother, as the devil does holy water."

They were by this time circling Candler Field, which seemed to be bustling with feverish activity—planes of various types were either landing, or else starting up; while several could now be seen cruising at sublime heights, either being put through their paces by pilots, or what was more likely carrying excursionists in the shape of "sandbags," greenhorn air holiday makers, out to get an experience that would give them a superior advantage over friends who had never as yet gone aloft.

Jack made an exceptionally clever landing, and then turned over the stick to his mate, as if eager to make it appear that Perk was the *real* article when it came to being the head pilot of the multi-motored cabin Fokker, that had not the least sign of a name, nor yet a number to identify it.

A number of men came running toward the rather retired spot where Jack had purposely come down. Leading them was a little whipper-snapper specimen, in a rather loud checkered suit, who gave all the recognized signs of being a hustling, live-wire newspaper man, always on the scent for some unusual happening such as could be turned into a thrilling story,—such keen investigators are to be found at nearly every airport worth while, eager to satisfy the curiosity of the multi-tude of readers who are developing air mindedness at a rapid rate.

"Greetings gents;" he started in to say, with a cheerful grin on his sharp features, and holding a pencil in one hand while he had a pad of blank paper all ready in the other. "If you would kindly give me a few facts connected with your identity, where you jumped off, whither bound, and so

forth the many readers of my paper would be glad
to extend to you a warm welcome to the Gate City
of the South."

Jack gravely shook hands with the diligent
worker, and obligingly fed him a little cock-and-
bull story, giving the names he and Perk had
recently taken upon themselves, and merely stating they were from Texas, bound to Atlanta on
private business connected with aviation circles.
He did this to quiet the news gatherer, until they
could dispose of their ship, and get started for the
hotel in a taxi to be hired near by.

Jack knew the breed to a dot, and felt confident
the lively chap would fill in enough imaginary
details to make an interesting account; so that
was that, and he was at liberty to turn to the one
in authority with whom arrangements could be
made for parking the big Fokker in a convenient
hangar at so much per diem.

Of course wise Jack had seen to it that never
the slightest clue could be discovered by the
shrewdest spy, to indicate what these air travelers
really had in view—he was quite willing that such
a sneaky investigator examine the ship from one
end to the other, and welcome—the gravest danger
of discovery would lie in some indiscreet remark
on the park of Perk; but even this did not give
Jack any considerable worry.

They were soon on their way into the heart of wide-awake, bustling Atlanta, and presently brought up at the noted hostelry, to which they had been directed to proceed.

Jack, after dismissing the taxi, followed the hotel attendant who had seized upon the two bags they had with them. He registered without ostentation; and no sooner had the clerk taken a look at their names, when about to assign them a double room on the third floor, than he remarked casually:

"A letter waiting for you, Mr. Warrington," and after shuffling a pack of envelopes swiftly, he handed Jack a registered letter, bearing the Washington postmark across the stamps.

Jack carefully deposited the same in an inner pocket; then a minute later they both followed a bellboy into the elevator and ascended.

When finally they found themselves behind a closed door Perk turned an eager face upon his comrade, as he remarked in a low tone, with a nervous look all around, as though half expecting to discover some eavesdropper peeping out from a closet, or from behind an easy-chair:

"She kim okay, seems like, Ja—er Mr. Warrington—then things they're keepin' on the move, an' we're a step closer to aour field o' operations than when we started aout, eh, what, suh?"

"Lock the door, brother—I'm going to get busy decoding this letter, after which you'll know *everything*. Now settle down in that chair, and give me ten minutes of time for the job—possibly a bit more, since I see it's rather a long communication."

Perk followed these directions out, and continued to watch the other as a terrier might hover over a hole in the kitchen wall, from which he expected a rat to thrust out his nose at any second.

Jack took a little more time than he had reckoned on; but, being expert at reading the secret cipher code adopted by the Government, in the end he had mastered the entire contents of the letter of instructions.

"Pull over this way a little, partner," he told the feverishly waiting Perk. "I want to lower my voice while explaining what it's all about; and we just can't be too careful, since walls sometimes have ears especially in this day of the hidden dictograph. To begin with," he went on to add, "we seem to have guessed fairly well that it was bound to have some connection with the smuggling business along the Atlantic seaboard, between Norfolk and Savannah."

Perk's grin was enormous at hearing this.

"Didn't I jest *know* that'd be aour job?" he chuckled, evidently vastly pleased at having "hit the target in the bull's eye." "Ever since we carried on so well daown in Floridy along back, I been 'spectin' Unc. Sam'd root out same kinder game fur us to get busy on onct more."

"But this promises to be the biggest adventure we've ever tackled, bar none, brother," Jack proceeded to explain. "This letter goes on to tell what an enormous amount of unlawful stuff is being flooded on the country through a powerful syndicate that's said to be backed by some heavy unknown parties with unlimited capital at their control. Ours is going to be the task of finding out who they are; and likewise throwing a monkeywrench into the smoothly running machinery by which they have been cheating the Government revenue right along, getting bolder and bolder, so that they virtually snap their fingers under Uncle Sam's nose."

"Gee! that sounds fine to me, ole hoss," gurgled Perk, rubbing his hands vigorously together as he spoke. "I jest kinder allers did yearn to tackle things sech as had a tough reputation behind 'em. Course there's been a wheen o' customs men atryin' to squash this combine—it's allers thataways, seems like!"

"Yes, looks as if the whole business is running true to form, brother," Jack further admitted. "The Chief candidly tells me they have been laying all sorts of clever traps for many moons, only to have these skip-by-night lads give them the laugh. He hopes we'll meet up with better luck."

"If so be it's a fair question, partner, haow do they reckon this traffic she's bein' kerried on, to slip by the fast customs patrol boats an' land the cargoes safe an' sound?"

"That's where the crux of the whole affair seems to come in," Jack thrilled the other by saying. "A few craft from Bimini have been overhauled, and seized, though as a rule the crew always managed to slip away, jumping overboard close in among the reeds, and disappearing in the brush along the river bank. But these occasional seizures never made even a dent in the immense operations, the Chief admits."

"How come then, buddy—bet yeou a cookey 'gainst thirty cents they got a line o' flyin' boats doin' the business."

"My stars! how wonderfully keen you are about guessing things; for that's just what this letter admits; and now we know why they called on us to get in the game—we seem to have made a big hit with the Chief, on account of how we managed to use our wings, and beat the Old Nick at his own game of high-spy."

"Ain't it great, though, to know they do 'preciate *somethin'* we've kerried aout? But what's the idee

o' aour headin' fur Charleston after we kick aout
o' this burgh, eh, partner?"

"There are a lot of things to be said and done
before we can break into the game; and we'll get
fully posted by the Government agent in Charleston. Besides, we've got to handle another kind of
ship,—in fact an amphibian, capable of dropping
down on water as well as on land, and taking off
the same way."

"Glory be! naow ain't that fine?" Perk exclaimed, ecstatically. "I never yet had anythin' to
do with them crocodile type o' boats, an' never
'spected to; so this same is a big s'prise, as well as
a pleasure—thank the Chief fur me whenever
yeou're writin', baby."

"Okay, brother," came the ready answer. "Fortunately it happens that I'm somewhat familiar
with the handling of that type of boat. Besides,
we're under orders not to hurry things along at all
—to take our own time, and get fully in touch
with our new craft before starting on the job for
keeps."

"Air we meanin' to handle this layout all by aour
lonesome?" Perk questioned.

"As a rule, yes; but we are also expected to call
upon certain skippers of fleet patrol boats to lend a
hand. He's given a list of four rum chasers whose
commanders will recognize the signal we give, and

place their craft at our disposal as long as we wish; so you see we're to really be in command of a squadron, if the necessity arises. I'm meaning to take down the names of the four customs boats before I destroy this illuminating letter, according to instructions."

Then Jack went on to speak of other things the letter had contained, with the intention of posting Perk regarding the immensity of the task being given over to their handling.

"He described this wide-stretching conspiracy to smash the Coast Guard service as a species of octopus, reaching out its myriad of arms, so as to cover the entire coast line—deliveries have been accomplished with almost clock-like regularity, and the custom service is being made a laughing stock among those in the secret. No wonder the Chief is feeling hot under the collar; for I reckon there never as yet has been a time like the present, when all the best laid plans of his most skillful and bravest men have gone on the rocks. I've a feeling that if we manage to give this big conspiracy its death blow, there isn't a favor too great for the Boss to grant us."

"What's bein' kerried in mostly, partner—does he tell us that?"

"He mentions expensive liquor, of course, as the principal contraband," Jack informed him "but narcotics as well have been coming, in un-known quantities, straight from China, also some country in the Balkans, Turkey being suspected. Then there are diamonds, and other precious stones that carry a heavy duty; laces; expensive Havana cigars from Cuban factories; and even Chinese immigrants, so eager to land in the country of Opportunity and dollars they are willing to pay enormous sums for transportation, with a safe landing guaranteed."

"The more the merrier, sez I," snapped Perk. "Yeou was asayin' a bit ago it's b'lieved they done got rafts o' spies pickin' up secrets o' the customs service, so's to trick the boats into startin' aout on false leads, that leaves the landin' places unguarded —mebbe, naow, ole scout, yeou even goes so far as to reckon that slick newspaper gink might be jest sech a peek-a-boo boy, aout to put the kibosh on aour fine game."

"You never can tell, buddy; if you meet him again play the deaf and dumb racket, which is the only safe plan."

CHAPTER III

THE LEECH HANGS ON

"Hot-diggetty-dig! seems like the more we poke into this here business, the warmer it gets!" Perk exploded, banking on the safety of their hotel room to keep his language from being heard.

"Oh! like as not all this is only the opening gun of our new campaign," was his companion's cool comment. "Later on, when we find ourselves neck deep in the mixup, you'll be looking back, and smiling at what you're saying now. From present indications I'd say this affair is giving promise of being the biggest case we ever had the nerve to tackle."

"The bigger they get the further they falls, partner, doan't make any mistake 'bout that ere fack," said Perk, grimly. "Huh! sometimes I get to thinkin' what happened up in that Hole-in-the-Wall outlaw retreat, and I'm awonderin' what ever did come o' that gang after we kicked off with aour prisoner."*

"Which reminds me I didn't think to tell you *all* the news that was contained in that letter from Los Angeles—want to hear it now, brother?"

*See *"Trackers of the Fog Pack."*

"Sure do, Mister," snapped Perk, greedily; "it'll amuse me while I'm awashin' up here in aour neat little bathroom."

Jack followed him into the next compartment, evidently so that he could keep his voice down to a low pitch.

"Something like a week later," he told the listening Perk, "they took off in the biggest crate they could commandeer into the service—half a dozen fighting men, heavily armed, and prepared for anything that might come along. Good weather favored them, and they came in sight of the valley among the high cliffs in the daytime.

"After circling, and lowering their altitude, they could not see the least thing to indicate the presence of a solitary human being; so finally the pilot set them down exactly on the smooth landing field the gang used when working their old wreck of a ship, carrying the packages of counterfeit notes out to distribute the same to different stations; and fetching back assorted supplies, including the best of grub.

"The place was abandoned, and looked like an earthquake had struck that particular quarter— the mouth of the pass leading into the wonderful valley was filled thirty feet high with a mass of rocks, thrown down by the tremendous force of the bomb you exploded when we cleared out; and some of the cabins and huts had been knocked to flinders by the men in their rage at being kicked out of their hidden retreat. Their old plane too, was scattered all around the field.

"The Government agents found the plates from which the spurious notes had been printed, and destroyed all but a portion, which they wished to forward to Washington for inspection by the Chief and his staff. Then they amused themselves by climbing to a five hundred foot ceiling, and making a target of the hut where the work had been carried on. Our friend in L. A. went on to assure me a clever hit by a bomb had scattered that squatty building we used to watch by the hour, to the four winds; and the printing press too was smashed to useless atoms by the force of the explosion."

"Bully! bully!" Perk was saying, joyously, proudly, through the soap lather he had accumulated on his face; "then we sure did a natty piece o' work up there in that God-forsaken neck o' the woods. Seems like life has got *some* bright spots in the framework arter all, an' ain't jest a dinky fogbelt like I sometimes find myself b'lievin'."

"It has its ups and downs we've got to remember, partner," advised sensible Jack; "especially along the risky line of business we're engaged in.

So we've got to take things as they come, wet weather mixed with sunny days, and just keep on doing our duty as we find it."

"Huh gue—reckon we gotter jest grin an' bear it," added Perk, rubbing his face and neck with the course huck towel, as he loved to do on occasion. "But haow long do we stick here in Atlanta tell me, Boss?"

"For one night only, if things work as I hope they will," said Jack, promptly enough, showing that his plan of campaign was beginning to shape up.

"Mind if I step aout for a little while, partner; I done forgot to lay in some tooth-paste, an' I'm kinder used to havin' a tube o' the same along with me, yeou know, suh?"

Perk was the possessor of an unusually fine set of teeth, of which he was inordinately proud, as Jack had occasion to know full well; so that this request on his part seemed perfectly natural.

"Certainly not, *Wally*," Jack told him, purposely emphasizing the name, as if to keep the other from forgetting how necessary it was to be forever on his guard, so as not to be caught napping. "Like as not you'll find a drugstore handy to the hotel, and can get what you want easily enough. I'd rather you didn't go far away—a walk might seem like a fine thing; but when it's taken I want to be

(155)

along, as two pair of eyes and ears might be better than one, to ward off danger."

"That's okay, Mister," came the cheery reply, as Perk stepped over to pick up his hat; "an' it gives me a warm feelin' 'raound my heart to hear yeou say that same—I'm never so happy as when goin' into action, yeou know right well. When I was over in France, helpin' run that sausage balloon we used for observation purposes, it allers gimme a wonderful thrill jest to see six Heinie ships takin' off, intendin' to ketch us guys 'fore we could drop to solid earth, an' knock the stuffin' aout o' us with some o' their consarned bombs, which they sure knowed haow to manufacture to beat the Frenchies all holler. So-long Ja—Mr. Warrington I'll be back agin in a jiffy."

Just the same it was fully fifteen minutes before Perk again showed up; and Jack found himself beginning to worry when the door opened, with Perk's grinning face exposed. Jack noticed that after the other entered the room his first act was to most carefully *lock the door*; and there was something significant about this action, so foreign to Perk's usual carelessness, that the other was forced to believe something or other must have happened while he was out of the hotel, to render Perk so solicitous.

"Got your tooth paste, did you, boy?" he asked.

"Easy enough," quoth Perk, still with that quiz-zical expression on his sun-tanned, homely face. "Found there was a drugstore right handy; an' seein' I was thirsty I jest stopped over to pick up a drink o' soda an' cream. That's where things begins to happen, yeou see."

"Oh! they did," echoed Jack, raising his eye-brows as he watched the face of the other, and noting how a grave look had succeeded the humor-ous one. "Suppose you tell me what it was came along while you were enjoying your soda?"

"Well, yeou see, partner," commenced Perk; "there happens to be a gink astandin' close by, which I aint paid any 'tention to, bein' wrapped up in my own affairs jest then. I'd raised the glass to take a fust sup when I done heard somebody say, right by my ear seemed like: 'Goin' to stay with us in Atlanta enny length o' time, Mister Corken-dall, suh?"

Perk evidently had a little streak of the dramatic in his composition, for he stopped just then, and eyed his companion eagerly, as if tickled to know his communication had given the usually cool Jack a bit of a start.

"Oh! you don't say, brother?" the other was remarking; "then after all the party at the soda counter wasn't quite a stranger to you seeing he evidently had learned your name?"

"Darned if I kin make aout partner, haow he ever got wise to the fack, so's to call me Mister Corkendall."

"Go on, brother—what did you do then?" demanded Jack.

"Huh! I was a bit flustered, yeou see," explained Perk, " 'cause I'd got a side squint at his mug; I reckoned I needed 'bout half a minute to git a grip on my senses; so I tilted up my glass, an' swallered a few times; and say it 'peared to me like a thousand things flashed through my poor ole brain like a stroke o' lightnin'."

"Did you answer him?" demanded Jack, frowning.

"I sure did," came unhesitating the reply; " 'case I jest had to. Yeou see, partner, he'd been astandin' thar right along, an' in course he done heard me order my drink; so if I tried to play that dumb trick, as haow yeou tole me, he'd aknown things must a been a bit mixed, an' the fat'd be in the fire. Did I do the right thing Boss, tell me?"

Jack smiled amiably again.

"That was certainly one time your mother wit *didn't* fail you, comrade," he told the other. "Now, go ahead and let me know what followed; because I've already guessed the man at your elbow must have been that Smart Aleck newspaper reporter we last saw looking over our ship so suspiciously."

CHAPTER IV

PERK HAS AN ADVENTURE

Perk might have been observed swelling out his chest somewhat, as though this praise on the part of his ally went straight to his head like rich wine.

"I done tole him it was all up to yeou, Mister Warrington—seein' as haow I was jest a humble air pilot aworkin' fur yeou—we might be in Atlanta a hull week, mebbe so, fur all I knowed."

"That was another clever thing for you to say, brother," Jack assured him, only too ready to praise when praise was due; "it might serve to throw him off the scent; but no matter how long or how short our stay chances to be, I've a hunch we're bound to see more than we want of that nosey chap. Like most of his breed he means to find out all he can, either to make a story that will give his readers a fine kick; or on the other hand, if he does happen to be one of that syndicate's paid spies, to learn who and what we really are, and why we're in Atlanta, coming out of the west—for I reckon he saw our first approach this same day, and jotted that fact down in his mind."

"He done tried hard to start me talkin' 'baout

yeour business, so I jest had to tell him as haow yeow was on'y sportin' fo' sport, an' undecided whether to go on daown to hunt black bears in the canebrakes o' Ole Louisiana; or else strike aout fo' Currituck Sound on the coast, to git a whack at the wild geese an' swans as kin be shot on the club preserves."

"You couldn't have done better any way you tried, brother," warmly commended Jack, whacking the other on his back, and causing him to fairly glow with satisfaction. "Only I hope he didn't catch on about that three distinct language business I was speaking about not so long ago."

Perk shook his head briskly in the negative.

"I was mighty keerful not to say *too* much, partner," he continued; "with him afirin' questions at me like the rat-tat-tat o' a machine-gun. So I pays fo' my soda, an' tells the youngster I gotter hurry back to where yeou was awaitin' fo' me to unpack the bags; an' with that I leaves him right whar he was standin', lookin' at me outen them sharp eyes o' hisn like he'd bore into me with a gimlet, so's to know ever'thing I had in my head. That sap is certain sure the mos' uncomfortable bird to run across when yeou got a secret up yeour sleeve, I ever did tackle."

"I can well believe you, brother," observed the relieved Jack. "Chances are you've left him in something of an uncertain frame of mind; but as he's built on the pattern of a bloodhound, he isn't meaning to give up the scent as long as we're within his reach. That forces me to decide on skipping from Atlanta as soon as possible, for he's marked 'dangerous—keep out.'"

"What's next on the programme, Mister?" asked Perk, satisfied to have come out of his little adventure with credit, and nothing like reproof from the pal whose good opinion he coveted so much.

"I must leave you here for an hour or so, and keep my appointment with Mr. Justice, although I hardly expect him to give me anything like the full details of the work ahead of us—that must wait until we get to Charleston, when everything will be laid before us; together with coast charts issued by the Government from surveys carried out by experienced geographers, and which we can rely upon to the fullest extent."

"I done reckons then, partner, yeou got yeour plans fixed up in case he is alayin' fo' yeou somewhars, eh, what?"

Jack chuckled as if amused.

"I understand how you're referring to our enterprising young scribe on one of Atlanta's lively papers; and especially vigilant in connection with air travel matters at Chandler Field—nothing would please me more than to take him on, and give him a whirl or so. I think I can play my part as a millionaire sportsman to the dot, and give him a mouthful that's apt to set him wondering more than ever. I might even invite him to dine with us, say tomorrow evening at the Grady here, when he will be at liberty to ask all the questions he wants about my love for outdoor sports, and so on—that would be a good joke on the slick lad, since we'll be on our way east many hours before that time."

"Gosh all hemlock! but say, wouldn't that be rich, though; an' what wouldn't I give to be close by, an' hear haow yeou stuffed the duffer," Perk went on to gush, surveying his companion with eyes that fairly glowed with sincere admiration.

"Lock the door, and under no consideration allow any one to enter while I'm away. Just say you're tremendously engaged, and can't be disturbed, if that everlasting busybody shows up."

"Huh! jest trust me to lay the same aout if he gets too fresh," grunted Perk with a menacing ring to his voice. "Course I wouldn't knock him any what yeoud call physically, only shut him up, an' send him off to mind his own business."

"When I come back we can have another little chin, for I promise to keep you fully posted from now on, concerning everything connected with the big game. After that we'll have a full dinner, and decide about pulling out of Atlanta while the going is good."

"Tonight, does yeou mean, partner?" queried Perk, craftily.

"Possibly, yes," came the ready reply. "We'll take a look over the afternoon *Journal,* and see what sort of flying weather is offered for the next twelve hours; and if at all favorable we can make our plans accordingly, so as to jump off before midnight. Candler Field is kept fully lighted nights, with so many ships of all types coming and going, on schedule and otherwise, that there'll be no difficulty about that part of the deal."

"Huh! which makes me remember I done got a copy o' that same paper when I was in the drug-store," explained Perk, pulling it out of his pocket as he spoke; "so I kin be amusin' myself while yeou're gone. I'll suck every bit o' weather information outen the paper, bet yeour boots, so's to be all primed when yeou come back; it'll be supper-time 'baout then, an' right naow I'm feelin' them grippin' pains daown below, sech as allers warns me the fires they need stokin', so's to keep the engine workin' full speed."

This arrangement pleased Jack perfectly; he realized how Perk was apt to be more or less "fidg-etty," and it was just as well he had something to read while standing guard over their luggage, so as to keep his mind from other subjects.

Jack waited outside for a brief space of time, and thus heard the key being duly turned in the lock, which relieved him of any further anxiety concerning the one left behind.

Perk, left to his own devices, settled down in an easy-chair to make himself comfortable. Beginning with the first page he read everything that had any promise of interest, applying himself particularly to such items as covered aviation matters. As is the case in these enlightened days of intense activity in air circles, he came upon a number of brief articles along those lines, all of which he absorbed with deepest interest.

Then for five or ten minutes he allowed himself to sit there, his mind filled with the magnitude of aerial inventions that had been sprung on the market within the last ten years; and marveled at the vast gap separating the bustling present with those lean years when he was serving his country over in France, attached to the observation corps, with their clumsy sausage balloons that could be let soar at a limited height, and then drawn down by rope and windlass when some enemy threatened their safety.

Arousing himself presently Perk next busied himself in searching the columns of his paper for the latest weather report, especially as concerned the promises for flying craft.

Eventually he found what he was after, and read the report most eagerly. To his delight it seemed to be favorable throughout the coming night, a fact of considerable importance to all air mail pilots, as well as others who were contemplating going aloft while the night lasted.

People passed the door of the room from time to time; and twice Perk had an idea some one was fumbling at the lock; but concluded it might have been some tenant of a neighboring room, either going out, or coming in, for at least nothing suspicious followed, and he breathed easy again.

The hour had just about slipped by when he caught footsteps he knew right well; as he listened he heard them stop before the locked door; then came a light tap, and he caught Jack's voice:

"Wally, it's me—Warrington, you know!"

"Okay, suh!" sang out the one within, as he stepped over and turned the key.

"How about it, partner—anything happened since I left?" Jack asked softly, after he had again turned the key in the lock.

"Not any, suh—an' I ketched the weather report in the dinged paper, which gives us the pleasin' information as haow it's bound to be halfway decent this same night, with wind from the southwest up at three thousand feet ceilin', which makes things look kinder promisin', I'd say, suh."

"That settles it then, buddy; we'll get a move on, and climb out before twelve. Might as well strike Charleston with as little delay as possible, for we'll possibly have to hang around that place some time, tuning up our new crate to know its possibilities. Besides, I've a feeling this town wont be big enough to hold both us, and that cub of a reporter, and keep him from whiffing some of our secrets with that inquisitive nose of his."

Perk grinned.

"Strikes me, partner, yeou done run up against that nosey critter, same like I done, aint that a fack, suh?"

Jack drew a card out of his vest pocket and tossed it on the table near which the pair of them were just then seated.

"That's the card he pressed into my hand, with the name of his sheet on the same. We've an appointment to dine with him here at the Grady to-morrow night, when he will be at liberty to ask as many questions as he pleases, connected with a rich sportsman's love for the game fields."

"Hot-diggetty-dig!" spluttered Perk, fairly aghast; but without waiting for him to say another word Jack continued, with a chuckle:

"Always providing we are still in Atlanta at

that time. Yes, I gave him a nice little run for his money—led him on interesting journeyings, and along pleasant ways. He fell for it all, as far as I could judge; and probably I managed to get the fish well hooked; but they're a slippery bunch, these newspaper chaps, and can give the best detective points, to beat him in the end in solving the great mystery. I'm leery of the whole tribe, partner—you never can tell whether you're stringing them, or they are playing you, giving you line so as to bring you up with a round turn eventually. We shake off Atlanta's dust by midnight, brother—and that goes!"

CHAPTER V

THEIR RUNNING SCHEDULE

"Hot-diggetty-dig! What a big snap I shore missed by not bein' jest 'raound the corner, alistenin' while yeou was afeedin' that tall yarn to 'im, what's the name o' that trail hound what builds up thrillin' yarns fo' the readers o' his paper to swaller?" and after taking a look at the card still lying on the table Perk continued: " 'James Douglas Keating,' huh! well, Jimmy, mebbe so yeou didn't run up 'gainst a buzz saw when yeou tackled aour—er, Mr. Rodman Warrington."

"Wait and see," cautioned Jack; "for all I can tell that lad may have been feeding me some slick medicine when he seemed to fall for my talk so readily. I'm not going to feel dead certain I scotched the busybody until we've left Atlanta and Candler Field well in our wake, with nothing happening to prove a give-away."

"Yeou would, partner—it'd be jest like yeou to say 'mebbe' till things they got ab-so-lutely certain —never yet knew yeou to jump at conclusions, so I done reckon yeou was really born to be a scientist. When do we eat, I'd like to know; things are agettin' near the danger line with me, right naow, an' there's a 'cry from Macedonia, come on an' dine.' "

"Let's go," Jack told him, reaching out for his head covering; for they had both doffed their flying clothes before quitting the ship, and were in ordinary garments that would not cause comment or unusual notice on the streets of any city.

Over a very bountiful dinner they continued to "talk shop" in low tones. Since their table was a bit removed from any other, thanks to Jack tipping the head waiter bountifully, with the orchestra playing softly, it seemed almost an impossibility for any hostile ear to catch a single word they uttered.

Thus Perk was put in possession of further valuable information with regard to the probable field of their forthcoming adventure, Jack having managed in his customary clever fashion to get hold of reading matter covering the entire romantic coast country between Norfolk and Savannah.

"It seems to be a wonderful section, just teeming with queer people and equally strange sights; and for one I'm a bit eager to look things over. Just the same, buddy, neither of us must forget even a minute the main object that's calling us into the coast skyways. We've got a man's size job on our hands, and some mighty smart people, as well as devil-may-care ones, to pack up against, so that a slip is apt to set us back, and for all we know even cost us our lives. I'm saying that not to scare any one, but because I've posted myself on the game, and know to what vile ends some of these dicks would go if they thought men of our trade were holding them under surveillance."

"Well, so be it, partner doant forgit I've heard the whine o' lead pills close to my ears many a time, so it's an ole story with me!"

"When we manage to get in touch with one or more of the swift Coast Guard patrol boats things will begin to look brighter—as though there might be something doing; but that wont come along for quite some time. We've got to get things down pat, know all about the regular routine movements of those swift airships, and then begin to cut into their number—first one must mysteriously disappear, and then a second, possibly even a third. By that time we'll have certainly thrown a pretty hefty scare into the bunch, and things are bound to slacken, more or less."

"Speed the day, sez I, partner caint come any too quick to suit me, an' that's no lie either," saying which valorous, fire-eating Perk again attacked his supper; for by this time they had reached the dessert stage, and were discussing prime apple pie, with the richest of thick cream to top it off, always one of Perk's favorites, when given his choice.

It will be noticed that when off duty these minions of the Secret Service were apt to live like kings, and with reason; for often they had to put up with scanty rations, and poor at that, when far removed from restaurant fare, and forced to live off the country. "First a feast, and then a famine," Perk was accustomed to saying when Jack mildly reproached him for giving so much thought to what he usually designated as "the eats."

Perk would have liked very well to have spent an hour or so at some theatre or other, and had even given a few hints about a screen play at the Paramount but met with no encouragement from his side partner.

"Best for us not to make any sort of an exhibit of ourselves while we're in close quarters with that write-up newspaper chap," he told Perk, who, realizing that Jack meant just what he said, allowed the subject to drop.

"Kinder gu——er-reckon as haow yeou're 'baout right there, ole hoss," he admitted, with a slight vein of regret in his voice; "course we kin see all the picters we want when we've struck the wind-up o' aour trail——that is, providin' we're still alive, an' kickin' as usual."

"That lad has got me guessing, and no mistake," Jack added; "in one way I admire such persistence, especially in one of his breed, where there's a big scramble for fresh news stories; but they can make it a whole lot disagreeable for other people in the bargain. Makes me think of the leeches that used to pester us by hanging on in the old swimmin' hole of my boyhood days—you just couldn't shake the blood-thirsty varments off, try as you might, they were such stickers."

Finishing their supper they strolled forth in a leisurely fashion, as if, as Perk himself observed in his quaint way: they had "the whole evening at their disposal, with nothing to do but kill time."

Picking up a late evening paper on the way to their room at the Henry Grady Hotel they settled down to be as comfortable as possible, until the time arrived to make a start.

"We'll get a taxi to take us out to Candler Field," quoth Jack, always arranging his plans with meticulous certainty; "then change to our flying togs, and get going as quietly as possible. It's to be hoped that sticking plaster wont be nosing around out there, to see some mail ship start off, or come into the airport—you never can tell about such fly-by-nights, who bob up in the most unexpected places just when you don't want to see them."

"Huh! yeou said it, partner," Perk added, whimsically; "jest like I used to see that queer jack-o'-lantern in the country graveyard foggy nights now here, an' agin over yonder, fur all the world like a ghost huntin' fur its 'ticular stone to climb under agin."

Jack, having made himself comfortable, commenced glancing over the paper he had picked up, briefly scanning each page as though skimming the news.

"Haow 'bout the weather reports, buddy?" asked Perk, later on, suppressing a big yawn, as though time was hanging somewhat heavily on his hands, being, as he always proudly declared, "a man of action."

"Just about the same as a while ago—no change in the predictions having come about," he told the other.

"Like to be no storm agoin' to slap us in the teeth, then, eh, what?"

"I don't see where it could come from, it being clear in almost every direction, saving possible rain in South Florida; so don't let that bother you in the least, old scout."

"An' fog—haow 'bout that same, suh? I opines as haow I sorter detest fog more'n anything I know—'cept mebbe stones in my cherry pie."

"No record of any fog over the air-route east,"

Jack informed him; "and you know we mean to follow the flash beacons all the way to Greenville, South Carolina, where they turn off in the direction of Richmond, while we shift more to the southeast by south, and head for Charleston. It looks as though we'd have a nice, even flight all the way, and land in our port early tomorrow morning—without trying to make any great speed in the bargain."

Time passed, and it drew near the hour they had selected for their leaving the hotel. Perk was a bit eager to be going, and began to pack his bag as a gentle hint to his running mate.

"Finish mine while about it, partner," he was told by his comrade; "while I'm down below settling our joint account, and securing a taxi. I'll be back in a short while; and then for business."

"Yeah! that strikes me where I live, buddy. Take yeour time, an' doant come back atellin' me that pesky Jimmy's squatted in the hotel lobby, alookin' over everybody as goes aout, er comes in."

Jack was gone as much as ten minutes, and then opened the door quietly, to have the other snatch a quick inquiring look at his face and say:

"Ev'rything lovely, an' the goose flyin' high, ole hoss?"

"We're going to kick off right away; and so far the coast seems clear."

CHAPTER VI

By the Skin of Their Teeth

Once settled down in the taxi Perk felt much better. He had been casting suspicious glances this way and that, eying a number of parties, as though he more than half anticipated the slick newspaper man might be hanging around the Grady in some clever disguise, bent on tracking them to the aviation field.

"Huh! kinder guess—ev'rything's okay with us naow—glad Jack didn't hear me asayin' that forbidden word, er he'd be kickin' agin. Tarnel shame haow a life-long habit do stick to a guy like glue —didn't realize haow things keep acomin' an' agoin' year after year, when yeou git 'customed to doin' the same."

Perk was muttering this to himself half under his breath as the taxi took off, and immediately headed almost straight toward the quarter where the fast growing Candler Field lay outside the thickly populated part of Atlanta.

He was just about to thrust his head out of the open upper part of the door on the left side when Jack jerked him violently back.

"Hey! what in thunder—"

"Shut up! and lie back!" hissed the other, almost savagely.

"Gosh-a-mighty! was *he* hangin' 'raound after all?" gasped the startled Perk, who could think of but one reason for the other treating him so unceremoniously.

Jack had turned, and was trying to see through the dimmed glass—he even rubbed it hastily with his hand as if to better the chances of an observation; but as they whirled around a corner gave it up as next to useless.

"It was *that boy* all right, and making straight for the hotel in the bargain; which proves he'd located our layout okay," he explained to the excited Perk.

"Doant tell me he done spotted us, partner?"

"I don't just know," came back the answer, hesitatingly. "I thought I'd yanked you back before he looked our way; but as sure as anything he came to a full stop, and stared after our taxi. For all we know he may be jumping for some kind of conveyance to follow at our heels."

"Hot-diggetty-dig! but things shore *air* gettin' some int'restin' like, I'd say, if yeou asked me, boy! An' even if he keeps on agoin' to the Grady the night clerk'll tell him as haow we done kicked aout. Kinder wish we was a zoomin' long on aour course, an' givin' Jimmy the horse laugh. Caint yeou git the shover to speed her along a little, ole hoss?"

"We're already hitting up the pace as far as safety would advise," Jack told him, as they both swayed over to one side, with another corner being taken on the jump. "It'd spill the beans if we had any sort of accident on the way to the ship; better let well enough alone, partner."

"Huh! the best speed a rackabones o' a taxi kin make seems like crawlin' to any airman used to a hundred miles an hour, an' heaps more'n that," grumbled the never satisfied Perk; but just the same it might be noticed that Jack did not attempt to urge the chauffeur to increase their speed at the risk of some disaster, such as skidding, when turning a sharp corner.

On the way Perk amused himself by taking various peeps from the rear, gluing his eye to the dingy glass. Since he raised no alarm it might be taken for granted he had made no discovery worth mentioning; and in this manner they presently arrived at the flying field, which they found fully illuminated, as though some ship was about to land, or another take off.

This suited them exactly, as it would be of considerable help in bringing about their own departure.

Jumping out Jack paid the driver, and after picking up their bags they hastened in the direction of the hangar in which they had been assured their ship was to be placed.

A new field service motor truck was moving past them, evidently bent on servicing some plane about to depart east, west, north or south; which Perk eyed with admiration; for he knew what a comfort it was to have one of these up-to-date contraptions swing alongside, and carry out all the necessary operations of fitting a ship out, which in the old days had to be done by hand, with the assistance of field hostlers.

"Anyhaow, we doant need a single thing to set us on aour way, which is some comfort," he remarked to his mate as they arrived at their destination.

While Jack was making all arrangements for their big Fokker to be taken out of the hangar, and brought in position for taking off, Perk continued to look eagerly around him, as usual deeply interested in all that went on in connection with a popular and always growing airport, of which Candler Field was a shining example.

"By gum! if there aint one o' them new-fangled air mail flags, painted on the fuselege o' that Southern Air Fast Express ship gettin' ready to pick off; an' say, aint she a beaut though—regulation wings in yellow, with the words 'U. S. Air Mail', an' the upper an' lower borders marked with red an' blue painted lines. Gosh! I'd be some proud naow to be handlin' sech a nifty ship in the service I onct worked by; but no use kickin', what I'm adoin' these days is heaps more important fo' Ole Uncle Sam than jest acarry'n' his letter sacks. An' mebbe that ship means to head back jest where we come from, Los Angeles, an' San Diego, by way o' Dallas, Texas. Haow they keep askippin' all araoun' this wide kentry, day an' night, like grasshoppers on a sunny perairie—the times o' magic have shore come to us folks in the year nineteen thirty-one."

Other sights greeted his roving eyes as he held himself impatiently in check waiting for Jack to give him the word to start. Both of them had hurriedly changed their clothes, and were now garbed in their customary working dungarees, stained with innumerable marks of hard service, yet indispensable to those who followed their calling.

It certainly did not take long for their ship to be trundled out on to the level field, and brought into position for taking off. There was considerable of a gathering, considering that it was now so late in the night; and Perk, giving a stab at the fact, came to the conclusion there was something out

of the common being, as he termed it, "pulled off"
—possibly the presence of that beautiful emblem
of the air mail service on the fuselege of the
western bound mail and express matter carrier had
to do with the occasion—a sort of honorary chris-
tening, so to speak—he was content to let it go
at that.

Jack was still talking with some one he seemed to
know, some one who must surely be a fellow pilot,
for he was dressed in regulation dingy overalls,
and kept hovering near that fine multi-motored
Curtiss Kingbird plane that he, Perk, understood
belonged to the new fleet of the line to be operated
in a short time between Atlanta and Miami,
Florida, carrying passengers, the mail, and express between the two airports.

Thus far there had been no sign of the ubiqui-
tous newspaper man, and Perk continued to bolster
up his hope this might continue to be the case to
the very moment of their departure. It would be
a bit exasperating should the fellow suddenly burst
upon them, jumping out of a taxi, and tackling
Jack with a beastly shower of questions that were
suited to the ends he had in view of building up
a fanciful story that must tickle the palates of the
numerous readers of his department on aviation in
the paper he served.

There, thank their lucky stars, was his companion giving the wished for call for him to stand by, as everything was fixed for immediate departure. In less than three minutes they would be taking the air, and leaving lighted Candler Field behind them—once that happy event had taken place and they could snap their fingers derisively at any attempt on the part of their determined annoyer to give them trouble.

"Huh! it's to be hoped the pesky guy doant take a notion to hire a ship, an' try to stick to aour tail, ashoutin' aout his crazy questions like he spected us to done hole up, an' hand him his story on a plate! Kinder gu—reckon as haow there aint much danger 'long them lines—it'd be a whole lot too hard fur him to manage. Okay, suh, right away!"

As Perk was supposed to be a pilot in the employ of Mr. Rodman Warrington, of course it was only right for him to be at the throttle of the ship when they took off. Accordingly he hastened to settle down in his seat where he could grip the controls, and manipulate things in the dash along the field that would wind up in a swing upwards toward the starry heavens.

Having given a last hasty inspection of his gadgets, and the numerous dials as arranged on the black dashboard before him, Perk called out, the propeller started to roar and spin like lightning; and in that very last second of time, as the ship commenced to leap forward, Perk caught a glimpse of the man whom they had believed left in the lurch—no other than Jimmy himself!

CHAPTER VII

On the Air-line to Charleston

Jimmy was leaping from a taxi that had come whirling almost up to the spot where their ship was in the act of taking off. Perk in that hasty look—when truth to tell he had no business to be taking his eyes away from his course ahead, lest he make a slip that would upset all their calculations—had seen the printer's ink man heading in leaps toward their plane—yes, and sure enough he was holding a pad of paper in one hand, and doubtless a sharpened pencil in the other, a typical up-to-the-minute knight of the press bent on snatching up his facts on the run.

Then Perk—still paying strict attention to his special task—gave a grunt of satisfaction, coupled with derision. To himself he must have been thinking, if not saying, "that's the time we jest made a slick get-away by the skin o' aour teeth—yeou're five seconds too late, Jimmy, boy—try some o' yeour tricks on slower game, not we-uns. Whoopla! here she goes!"

As they were just then about to leave the ground and start their upward climb of course it was absolutely out of the question for the one holding the stick to twist his head around so as to see what their tormentor was doing; but then he felt certain Jack must be taking in everything that occurred, and in good time he would be told of each little incident.

Perk had his instructions, and knew just what he was doing. Accordingly, when the ship had reached a comfortable ceiling of say half a thousand feet, he banked, and swung around so as to head toward the southwest.

"Shore thing," Perk was telling himself, in a spirit of pride and astuteness. "Sense the gent's is aimin' to git a black bear in them canebrakes o' ole Louisiana, we gotter be headin' thataways at the start. Hoopla! aint it jest the limit, apullin' the wool over the eyes o' one o' the darnedest sharpest newspaper boys as ever was?"

It had been arranged that they were to keep on that course for a brief time, and when sufficient distance had been covered—so that the hum of their exhaust could no longer be heard at Candler Field—they would change to another quarter, swing around the distant city, pick up the light at Stone Mountain, and from that point industriously follow the beacons that flashed every ten miles or so all the way to Richmond, Virginia.

Jack soon displaced his assistant pilot at the controls, and Perk was able to take hold of other special duties, such as were usually left to his direction.

One of the very first things he carried out was to attach the harness of the invaluable telephone, that, when connected with their ears allowed of such exchange of views as they saw fit to indulge in; and Perk was burning up with eagerness to find out what Jack must have seen after they made their start.

The big ship was speeding at a merry clip, and before long Stone Mountain would be reached with the first beacon flashing its welcome light to beckon them on their well marked course.

"Was that *him* as I guess—reckoned I done seed, jest as we started to move, hey, partner?" Perk demanded; and as Jack knew only too well he would have no peace until he handed over such information as he possessed, he lost no time in making answer.

"No other, brother—he came in a taxi, and was in such a hurry it's plain to be seen he'd picked up a clew at the hotel that sent him whooping things up, and burning the minutes until he got there at Candler Field. Unfortunately—for Jimmy —he dallied a half minute too long, trying to get some lead from that night clerk, and so we slipped one off on him."

"Yeou doant reckon as haow he'd be so brash

as to hire a ship, to try an' sit on aour tail, do yeou, ole hoss?" demanded Perk, who had even looked back once or twice, as though such a possibility had begun to bother him.

"Not a Chinaman's chance of such a happening, Wally—we've got a clear field ahead of us, and I feel pretty certain that's the last we'll see of our friend Jimmy. Just the same, leave it to him to concoct a thrilling yarn to feed to his readers tomorrow morning—imagination will supply the missing facts; and I'd like to set eyes on what he hatches up."

"Me too, partner," echoed Perk, greedily; "an' if it's possible while we hang aout araound Charleston I'm meanin' to look up all the Atlanta papers, and read all the air news they carry."

"Go to it, partner; but that must be Stone Mountain over there on our larboard quarter; look sharp, and you'll glimpse a flashing light, for we're about to pick up our first beacon."

"Bully for that, 'cause afterwards it'll be the softest sailin' ever, with aour course charted aout fur us most all the way."

"I'm holding her down a bit," explained Jack, "because we'd better stick to the beacons until dawn; after that we can depend on our compass and chart to carry us the rest of the way to Charleston."

"I get yeou, ole hoss, an' agree with yeou to a hair. No hurry whatever, yeou done tole me the Chief sez in his cipher letter o' instructions—slow an' sure, that's agoin' to be aour motto this campaign," and Jack must have chuckled to hear the impetuous Perk say that, it was so foreign to his customary way of rushing things.

The line of beacons was now picked up, and Perk could see sometimes as many as three at the same time—the one they were passing over; that left behind shortly before; and still a third faint flash at some distance beyond.

They had climbed to a ceiling of some two thousand feet, which might still be increased when passing over such outspurs of the Allegheny or Smoky Range Mountains as would be met on the regular air mail course to Richmond.

As the air seemed unusually free from any vestige of fog, being very clear, of course visability was prime, which fact added to Perk's happiness, he being unduly fond of such favorable weather conditions.

Such a voluble chap could not keep silent long, when it was so easy to chat with an accommodating companion; and hence presently Perk found something else to mention to the working pilot.

"I say, partner," he sang out, "tell me who yeour friend was, the pilot I seen yeou talkin' with, an' who sure seemed to be 'quainted with yeou."

· "Knew you had that question up your sleeve, buddy," Jack replied, always ready to satisfy any reasonable amount of curiosity on the part of his chum. "Yes, he was an old friend of mine, and I expect you've heard me speak of him more than a few times—one of the most adept pilots connected with the Curtiss people,—no other than Doug Davis, who back in twenty-nine won the country's speed race at Cleveland, with a record of a hundred-and-ninety miles an hour."

"Gee whiz! haow I'd liked to amet up with him!" exclaimed Perk, showing a trace of keen disappointment in his tone.

"I'd have introduced you, partner, only the conditions wouldn't admit it." Jack threw out as a bit of apology.

"But, say—what if that speed hound, Jimmy, happened to learn he was atalkin' with yeou, wouldn't your friend Doug be apt to give us away, withaout knowin' the reasons why we wanted to keep shady right naow?"

Jack gave him the laugh.

"Not on your life, buddy," he announced, without hesitation; "I managed to let Doug know what line I was in, and how just at present I'm a New York millionaire sportsman and aviator, Rodman Warrington by name, headed toward some shooting-grounds for a whack at big game. He's a lad you could never catch asleep at the switch; and make up your mind our secret's as safe with him as anything could be. Jimmy'd have all his trouble for his pains, if he ever tried to pump Doug Davis, who's as keen as they make them in our line."

"But, partner, didn't he introduce yeou to another pilot—I reckon I seen him adoin' that same, an' heow yeou shook hands with the other guy."

"Yes, but I'd already tipped Doug off, and he strung his friend with the story we've hatched up about our meaning to try the shooting in those wonderful canebrakes in Louisiana. And that's all he'll ever tell connected with my identity, till the cows come home, or water runs uphill."

"An' who did the other chap happen to be, if it's a fair question, suh?" continued Perk, who, once he started on an investigating tour, never would let go until he had extracted every particle of information available.

"Sorry that I didn't catch his name clearly; but Doug told me he was connected with the U. S. Air Reserve Corps operations functioning there at Candler Field," Jack explained

He certainly stirred up something when he said that.

"Well, well, what dye know 'baout that naow,"

gushed Perk, apparently thrilled more or less by
what he had just heard. "I've been gettin' wind
o' that ere movement, and meanin' to look it up
whenever the chanct drifted along."

"A most interesting subject, buddy, and one I'd
think you'd want to look into, seeing you're a
veteran of flying in the Great War over in France,
and could join without any trouble. From what
Doug told me, and what I've read concerning the
game, the organization is growing stronger every
day—made up of men especially fitted to step in
and man fighting planes, should any occasion arise,
such as another foreign war. Right in the southeast district there are something over two-
hundred-and-thirty pilot members, who could be
mustered by Uncle Sam in an emergency, just
twenty-two of whom belong in Atlanta, Doug
told me."

"Whee! haow fine that'd be fo' a feller o' my
makeup," Perk chortled, in glee. "I done gue—
reckons, suh, as haow they may have meetin's, an'
all that sorter thing—how 'baout it, partner?"

"That's one of the necessary things about the
Air Reserve Officers Corps," continued Jack who
evidently considered the organization an especially
fine thing for the airminded public to support.
"All through the winter they meet twice a week in
classes, to keep up with modern military and
aviation activities; and they get their new up-to-

date flying experience by taking off in one of five army training ships kept ready in the new reserve hangar at Candler Field—these are an Oil Curtiss Falcon regular attack plane; a 2-B Douglass dual control basic training ship, with 450 horsepower engines; and three other primary training ships. All the equipment connected with the Fourth Corps hangar is at Atlanta headquarters,—so Doug told me, and he ought to know if any one does."

"Gee whiz! an' to think o' what I been missin' all this time," moaned poor Perk, disconsolately. "Mebbe though it wouldn't ever do to apply fo' admission to such a organization, 'jest 'cause we-uns gotter to hid aour light under a bushel, while serving aour Uncle Sam in his ole Secret Service. Dye know I got half a mind to throw it all up, an' go back to carryin' the air mail, when a guy could show his own face, an' not live under a dark cloud;—but not so long as *yeou* sticks on the job, partner, I doant break away ever."

CHAPTER VIII

SHIPS PASSING IN THE NIGHT

They were by this time fully embarked on their night flight. Perk continued to watch the flash beacons as though they fascinated him, more or less.

"What I'd call a big snap, if anybody asked me," he kept telling himself from time to time. "Huh! when I was an air-mail pilot fur a short time, things wasn't so dead easy—not a blamed light on earth or in the sky, nawthin' but black stuff every-which-way yeou looked. Naow the guy at the stick jest keeps afollerin' a string o' blinkin' 'lectric lights that point aout his course fur him. Purty soft, I'd call it, an' no mistake either."

When they were passing directly over one beacon that kept blinking at them apparently, with about ten seconds between each flash, he could by turning his head, see a far-away swirling gleam marking the light in their rear; while dead ahead another, equally distant, kept up an enticing flash as though bent on assuring them everything was "all right."

"Jest one thing still wantin' to make these here air-mail boys right happy," he told himself;

"which is a ray to beat the danged fog that mixes things up like fun. When some wise guy finds a way to send a ray o' light through the dirty stuff, so's yeou kin see a mile away as if the air was clear as a bell, then flyin' blind is agoin' to lose all its terrors to the poor pilot. I shorely hopes to see the day that's done."

Later on Perk suddenly made a discovery that gave him a little fresh thrill—there was some sort of queer light almost dead ahead, that he fancied moved more or less; at any rate it was steadily growing brighter, beyond any question.

"Hot-diggetty-dig!" he muttered, still watching critically, as if hardly able to make up his mind concerning its meaning. "Looks mighty like a shootin' star; but then I never did see one that didn't dart daown, like it meant to bury itself in the earth. Must be a ship aheadin' this way—mebbe a mail carrier goin' to Atlanta to land on the same Candler Field we jest quitted—yep, that's what it is, with a light in the cabin to keep the passengers from worryin'—sandbags ain't any too joyful when they got to sit in the dark, with the ship hittin' up eighty miles an hour."

Having thus settled the identity of the strange moving light, Perk hastened to inform his mate of the discovery he had made.

"Ship's agoin' to pass us in the night, buddy,"

he called through the aid of the indispensable ear-phones. "Yeou kin lamp the light straight ahead naow."

"Yes, I'd already noticed the same, partner," came steady Jack's answer, as if he were not in the least disturbed, or excited by the occurrence.

"Gee whiz! but I shore hopes we doant meet head on, an' crash," ventured Perk, really to coax his chum to express an opinion, and thus reassure him.

"No danger of that happening, old scout!" snapped Jack; "but I'll veer off to starboard a bit, to make doubly sure against a possible collision. Strike up our cabin light, boy, so's to put them on their guard."

Of course they could not catch the slightest sound to corroborate their opinion, since their own ship was making so much racket. The light came closer and closer; at the same time Jack felt positive the other aerial craft must be following his own tactics looking to safety, and steering somewhat to the right, as discretion demanded.

Perk had snatched up a kerosene lantern and hastily lighted the wick. This he now moved up and down, then swung the same completely around his head, as though he thus meant to give the other pilot a signal in the line of fellowship and aerial courtesy.

Thus the two ships passed not three hundred feet apart, yet only vaguely seen by watchful eyes. Then they were swallowed up in the gloom of the night, the moon being under a passing cloud at the time.

"Fancy aour meetin' in space," Perk was saying, as though rather awed by such a circumstance; "it couldn't happen again in a month o' blue moons, aour comin' to grips thisaway, with millions o' miles all 'raound us, an' nawthin' but chance to guide both pilots."

"You're on the wrong track again, partner," Jack hastened to tell him. "Chance had little to do with this meeting; but that chain of brilliant flash beacons was wholly responsible. Just like two trains passing on a double-track railroad line— both airships were following the same marked course, and couldn't hardly miss meeting each other. In these latter days flying has become so systematized that the element of chance has been almost wholly eliminated from the game."

That remark kept Perk silent for some little time, the subject thus brought up was so vast, so filled with tremendous possibilities, he found himself wrestling with it as the minutes crept on.

So, too the night was passing by degrees, with their reliable Fokker keeping steadily on its way, putting miles after miles in their wake. Perk found himself growing more and more anxious for the first streak of coming dawn to show itself far off in the east, where the sun must be climbing toward the unseen horizon, and daylight making ready to disperse the cohorts of night.

Still it was always possible for him to make out the next beacon, with the aid of his binoculars, if he happened to be using them, as was often the case.

An hour and more after their "rubbing elbows" (as Perk termed it,) with the south-bound air-mail plane, once more Perk caught a suggestive beam of light ahead that told of yet another aircraft afloat, and advancing swiftly toward them, only at a much lower altitude.

"Naow I wonder who *that* guy kin be," he mused, while watching the light grow steadily larger. "Some kinder big ship in the bargain; but hardly one o' the mail line, 'cause they doant run 'em in doubles the same way. Hi! there, partner, we got a second neighbor, agoin' to pass under us in a minit er so. Jest a bit to the left—no danger o' bangin' noses this time, seems like. Gettin' to be thickly populated, as the ole pioneer settler said when a new fambly moved in 'baout ten mile off. Mebbe we'll live to see the day when the air o' night'll be studded with movin' lights thick as the stars be—looks thataways to me, anyhaow."

Again he signaled his good wishes with his

lantern, showing as much glee as a schoolboy whirling around his first fire spitting Roman candle, on the night of the Glorious Forth.

"Gee whiz! looky, partner—they're answerin' me, as shore's yeou're born! This is gettin' somewhere, I'd say; an' I'd give thirty cents to know who that guy might be."

"Just as well there's no way to exchange cards," sensible Jack told the excited one. "Never forget for a minute, partner, who and what we are; and how it's a prime part of this business to keep our light hidden under a bushel right along. Others flying for sport, or carrying on in commerce, may get a thrill from exchanging names, and hobnobbing with each other; but all that stuff is strictly taboo with men of the Secret Service."

"Squelched again!" Perk told himself, with one of his chuckles; "an' jest as always happens, Jack, he's in the right—I'm forgettin' most too often what goes to make up a successful officer of the Government, 'specially in aour line o' trade. Guess—I mean I reckons as haow I'll have to subside, and take it aout in thinkin'."

Perk was certain they must have long since passed over the eastern extremity of Georgia, and were even then swinging along with South Carolina soil beneath them. Yes, and he began to figure that he could detect the faintest possible rim of light commencing to show up far off to the east, as though dawn could not be far away.

"Huh! aint agoin' to be many more o' them bully flash beacons lightin' us on aour course," he was telling himself. "Chances air we'll be bustlin' over aour objective right soon; when it's goodbye to the air-mail route, an' us a turnin' aour noses near due south, headin' fo' Charleston on the seaboard, when the real fun is slated to begin. Caint come any too quick fo' a boob that answers to the name o' Gabe Perkiser. Yeah! that line is gettin' some broader, right along, which tells the story as plain as print."

Shortly afterwards he picked up a myriad of gleaming lights, that proclaimed the presence of a city of some magnitude; evidently the first sector of their flight had been reached, with a change in their course indicated.

CHAPTER IX

WHEN THE DAWN CAME

"Kinder looks like we'd hit civilization again, eh, ole hoss?"

With the dawn coming along thus high up above the surface of the earth, it was still night down below, save where numerous electric lights, on the streets, and along the railroad lines, especially within the limits of the yards, dispelled the shadows. Some of these were continually shifting; and since Jack had dropped down latterly until they were not more than five hundred feet above the level ground, only for their hearing being overwhelmed by the noise of their own speeding ship, they might have easily heard the puffing of switching engines, together with the rumble of many freight cars, possibly the loud whistles of some factory warning its employees it was time for them to be thinking of getting their breakfast, preparatory to another long spell in the cotton mills, or other places of labor.

"Here's Greenville, where we strike off on our own," Jack announced, as he made a right turn, and depending entirely upon the needle of the compass, took up a new line of flight—no signalling for switches, puffing of a steam engine for a start, nothing save a turn of the wrist; and without the least friction the airship was heading in the direction of Charleston, still far distant as the crow flies.

The lights began to grow dim in their rear, and before long the last vestige of the bustling South Carolina city faded out of sight.

But undoubtedly the dawn was steadily advancing, so that already Perk had been able to get fugitive glimpses of the ground they were so steadily passing over. He knew he would be feeling better when able to watch the panorama spread out like a vast chart under the swiftly speeding air craft, with towns, villages, and hamlets following in each other's train; the country itself dotted with innumerable cabins occupied by negro workers of the wide stretching plantations, where cotton, corn, and perhaps tobacco, would appear to be the staple crops harvested.

It was indeed worth while watching when daylight came upon the surface of the earth, and the sun could be seen in all his glory by those who had the privilege of an elevated observatory.

Perk settled himself down for a period of "loafing," having no particular duties needing attention. His main thought was concerned with the fact that they were swiftly passing over South Carolina, and getting closer to their main objective, where the remainder of their orders would be handed over to them as per prearranged agreement.

He indulged in numerous speculations as to just when and how Jack would make his attack upon the entrenched forces of the defiant clique, latterly giving Uncle Sam so much bother; and persisting in their thus far successful smashing of the patrol boat blockade along the coast, through the agency of numerous swift air smuggling craft—how many there might be Perk had no knowledge.

Well, just wait until he and his best pal got fairly started in the good work, and possibly some of those defiant pilots would be numbered among the "has beens," having mysteriously vanished from the ken of their fellow law-breakers.

"I shore doant want to brag," Perk told himself, as modestly as he could find the heart to be; "but jest the same I been along with Jack more'n a few times, when we run up agin sech gay birds; an' it was allers the same ole story over an' over agin. Right naow a good many cells in Atlanta, Leavenworth, an' a few more penitentiaries air filled by lads what reckoned nawthin' could beat 'em at their pet game; yet there they be, behind stone walls, an' nary one chanct in a thousand to break away. Huh! hope hist'ry repeats in this new adventure we're right naow embarkin' on, that's all."

Such confidence in a comrade bordered on the sublime, yet according to his light Perk felt he was justified in believing Jack to be at the head of his class—without a peer, yet modest withal, shrinking from praise, and content to let the heroes of unsurpassed air flights, as well as all manner of broken records for speed, endurance, and like exploits, bask in the spotlight, while he was satisfied to do his full duty, and afterwards remain unknown to fame.

Jack apparently still had a little fear lest something his best pal managed to do, when off his guard, might throw all their labors into the discard. On this account, and because they were now bearing down close to an important point in their schedule, he took occasion to once more delicately hint along such lines.

"For perhaps the last time, partner," he went on to say, soberly; "we've both got to get a firm grip on ourselves, and try to actually *live* the parts we're about to play. Let's consider we're actors, with a critical audience in front, watching closely to see if we leave any break back of which our real character may be seen."

"Huh! I like thataway o' puttin' it, Big Boss," snorted Perk, without the slightest hesitation; although he must have suspected that Jack was trying to impress this point particularly on his, Perk's mind—"I'll try my darnedest to keep a-thinkin' a thousand eyes and ears they be on to me, searchin' fo' some knothole in the fence to peep through, an' gimme the laugh straight. Go on an' say some more 'long them lines, buddy—I kin stand it okay."

"An actor to be a success must have the power, the ability to throw off his own ways and character, to assume whatever queer quirks marking the role of the person he is pretending to be. Try and forget you were Yankee born, and swap places with a son of Dixie, filled with veneration for those heroes in gray, soldiers of Lee, Jackson, Forrest, and all the other leaders of the sacred Lost Cause. You can do it, I'm dead certain, if you keep your mind steadfastly on that business alone, and forget a lot of other less essential matters."

"Shore I kin, an' I mean to, partner—yeou wait up an' see haow I'll pull the wool over their eyes— I'm Wally Corkendall, an' I was borned an' brought up in Birmin'ham, where them bully stories o' the colored folks that make yeou laugh like fun keep acomin' from right along. Yessuh! I done tole yeou I may be a man o' the world; but Dixie is my dwellin'-place, Birmin'ham my ole hometown."

So Jack let it go at that, and indulged in the hope his pal would not fall down in a pinch—it meant a matter of life and death with them, in view of the desperate type of men with whom they would soon be at close grips.

CHAPTER X
READY TO STRIKE

Up to then everything had been comparatively simple; but the worst was yet to come. They could not do more than guess as to the nature of the dangers and difficulties lying in ambush to trip them up. For aught they knew long weeks, crowded with perils and narrow escapes, would be their portion; with the crowning possibility of final disaster hanging over their heads day and night.

It was this uncertainty that made their job all the more attractive and thrilling to the comrades —in particular to Perk, whose restless soul seemed never to be content to loll in idleness and safety; but yearned to meet up with all manner of weird scrapes, that for the time being satisfied the burning desire of his feverish blood.

Perhaps that was his heritage, coming down from those ancestors who settled in New England, at the time America was a British colony; and when dread of Indian massacres kept every one's blood keyed up to the extreme; then again it might be Perk got it from his contact with the front line trenches in the Great War, where he may have been gassed, wounded, and lived the horrible existence that so many of our gallant boys did in the fierce battles of the Argonne—himself, he never bothered his head to figure out whence the feeling came—he only knew he had it, and fairly reveled in what he was pleased to term *action*; but which really stood for deadly peril.

It can thus be seen how Perk was making his life work along the right line for one of his disposition; since it would be difficult indeed to mention any other vocation where a man would do his daily stunt face to face with some calamity.

He continued to look down at the checkerboard below, admiring this, grunting his disgust at another spectacle, and many times glancing impatiently at his wrist-watch, as though he could thus hasten the hour and minute when they would be landing at their present destination.

Jack, on his part, while carrying out his ordinary duties as pilot, was running over in his active mind the various duties that must await their reaching the landing field in Charleston.

First, after seeing their ship safely stowed away in a convenient hangar—where it would stay until needed again, if ever—he must call at the post office for any letters that might have been sent on—under his assumed name, of course; after which it would be his business to drop in upon the Government agent, from whom he would receive further secret instructions, as well as every scrap of information possible, such as would be of assistance in laying out and following up their plan of action.

It pleased Jack to know how every detail was being carried out with the prime motive of abject secrecy—for instance, he had been instructed *never* to call at the office of the revenue official, since spies might have it under surveillance, and hold such a swell caller under suspicion—on the contrary the gentleman's private residence had been mentioned as the place of meeting; and the secret cipher of the Department must be invariably used should an exchange of letters become necessary.

He was to call at the house in the capacity of a distant relative of Mr. Casper Herriott in the city while *en route* to other places along the Atlantic seaboard, especially in the way of shooting grounds; he being a famous sportsman—Perk was not only his dependable pilot, but a skillful guide as well, fully acquainted with most of the sporting grounds of the great sounds and bays along North and South Carolina shores.

Jack found himself smiling to remember how his companion had at one time delicately hinted that since the Government had been so kind as to supply them with all manner of lovely guns, ammunition, and even shooting clothes and tempting high leather boots, all costing rafts of money, it might be possible for them to better carry out their assumed characters by indulging in a little foray among the canvasback ducks, mallards, and even wild geese—also remarking how it would be much too bad if, having been given the name, they might not also grab a handful of the game!

Already had Jack commenced to take copious notes, mental, as well as written down in his new notebook—in the secret code of course—and he expected to add copiously to this record after he had interviewed Mr. Herriott, and drank in all that gentleman would have to tell him.

Besides that he would try to paint a complete chart on his mind, covering the lay of the land along the coast, its innumerable indentations covering the shores of the great Sounds, Albemarle, Pamlico and others—also that section of swamps and morasses lying further south, where he already strongly suspected the main part of their work awaited them.

Already he had pored for hours over the Government Geographical Coast Survey charts, which, with others were contained in the waterproof case aboard the ship, and had proven their worth on a number of previous occasions; but as he could

not hope to always have these at hand for refer-
ence, Jack meant to carry along a mental picture
of the entire region, a feat impossible, save to him
whom the gods had favored with a wonderfully
retentive memory, made next to perfect from long
practice.

Up to then the most that Jack knew in connection with his work was that it must mean the shat-
tering of a gigantic conspiracy, backed by a number of wealthy but unscrupulous citizens; who
probably depended upon some real or fancied
"pull" to get them through in safety if they
were ever indicted, which they had every reason
was next to impossible.

The scope of this league, Jack also understood,
was almost boundless—all manner of efforts were
being put into practice daily, in order to cheat
Uncle Sam out of his "rake-off" upon various
dutiable foreign goods—diamonds, other precious
stones on which the Treasury Department levied
high sums when imported openly; rich laces; high
priced Cuban cigars, and a multitude of similar
goods mostly small in bulk, that could be easily
transported undetected aboard swift airplanes,
making secret landings amidst the almost untrod-
den wilds of that eastern shore!

Then there must be a continuation of the old
smuggling game—that of fetching cargoes of the

finest wet goods obtainable at some station of the West Indies; only the landing places had been transferred from the vicinity of Tampa and Miami, when those ports were too heavily policed to admit of taking the desperate chances involved; and were now transplanted to South Carolina territory, where they seemed to be working without the slightest molestation, with a daily flood of stuff being safely landed.

It was hinted that this powerful rival of the Government was going even a step farther—carrying undesirable aliens from Cuba across to the land they were so eager to reach, that they paid enormous sums for the privilege of being flown across the stretch of salt water—these were not only Chinamen, but Italians as well, criminals who had been chased from their own country by the alert Facist authorities as enemies of the realm, and saw in rich America the Mecca where they could soon acquire great wealth at easy pickings by eventually becoming beer barons, racketeers, and the like; after passing through a brief school course as ordinary bootleggers, and hi-jackers.

"Some job, believe me!" Jack summed up his reflections by saying, drawing in a long breath at the same time; and then following it all up with a laugh, as though even such a monumental task failed to dismay him.

"Cap, I kinder reckon we're right smart near Charleston, to jedge from thet bank o' smoke lying on ahead. I been keepin' tabs o' the miles we left behind us, an' it shore do tally with the distance marked on yeour map."

"I feel certain you're okay when you mention that same, matey," Jack assured the other; which commendatory remark caused Perk to look as pleased as a child when handed an all-day lollypop to suck on.

"Hot-diggetty-dig! it makes me happy to know as haow the waitin' game's 'baout all in naow, an' we're agwine—haow's that, buddy—to jump into action, and then more action. Me, I'm some hungry, partner; but mebbe it aint wise to take a snack when we're so clost to aour airport, with a landin' comin' along soon, an' real restaurant eats aloomin' up in the bargain."

"Try to hold your horses for half an hour or more, and I promise that you'll be filled up to the limit, regardless of expense. And now begin to live, breathe, and act as a Dixie bred man would do, ready to knock anybody flat who'd be so brash as to say one insulting word about your native Southland."

"The finest country God ever did make, barrin' none, suh; and don't yeou forgit it; but I kin see the airport a'ready, partner, off to the left a bit."

CHAPTER XI
WHERE WAR ONCE BROKE OUT

Shortly afterwards the two adventurers found themselves looking down at as entrancing an air picture as it would be possible to conceive; with Charleston Harbor stretching out to its furtherest extent before them.

"See that island over yonder, partner," said the admiring Perk, pointing as he spoke; "I kinder—reckons naow as haow that might be where ole Fort Sumter stood, durin' the war 'tween the States—yeou knows weuns daown hyah allers speaks o' that little flareup that way, 'stead o' callin' it the Civil War."

"So I understood, Wally, and I'm glad to find out you're so well posted on such facts, as it strengthens your position considerably. When you're in Dixie it's just as well to follow the crowd, and do as all true Southerners do."

It was a charming morning, the air "salubrious," as Perk said more than once, and everything seemed favorable to the success of their great undertaking— as far as they had gone, which was not anything to boast of.

Perk had already pointed out the landing field they were aiming to patronize, and of course the pilot circled the stretch several times, as he began to lose his altitude.

There was but little wind, and that favorable for making a successful landing. Then, too, a number of men had started to run toward the spot where indications pointed to their touching the ground, so they would not lack for any assistance required.

But Jack swung a trifle, and made contact shortly ahead of the foremost runner; the gliding, bumping ship gradually came to a complete stop, and both of them had hopped out of their cabin by the time several runners, breathing heavily from their exertions, reached the spot.

Jack was as suave and smiling as ever, a faculty that always made him "hail fellow well met" with most people. He picked out a party bearing the appearance of one in authority, and who, seeing his friendly nod, hastened up, holding out his hand with real Southern warmth.

"Welcome to Charleston, suh," he observed as they clasped hands, evidently understanding that the new arrival was not familiar with the ground, being apparently a stranger to the airport; which in itself was nothing remarkable in these days of fast increasing aviation strides, with new people coming and going on the up-to-date airways almost every day.

"My name is Warrington, and I am from New York City, down here for the shore shooting. This is my pilot and guide, Wally Corkendall, from Birmingham, Alabama. I wish to set my Fokker in a safe hangar for an indefinite space of time, for we shall have to make use of an amphibian during our month of sport, as it will be necessary to make many a night's camp on the waters of your wonderful bays and rivers. Would you kindly put me in touch with the party who has charge of such arrangements; I should expect to pay a week in advance and continue the same during the time of my stay."

That could be easily arranged, since it happened he himself was in charge of all such matters, the gentleman courteously informed his new guest; apparently sizing Jack up as a young man of wealth, willing to pay the price, no matter how much it cost, in order to enjoy himself to the utmost.

So the ship was properly housed, and Jack took pains to observe a lock on the doors, for which one of two keys was handed to him later on, after he had stepped over to the office, and finished arrangements by paying the sum agreed upon.

"Anything we can do to help make your stay in

our city pleasant, suh, you can depend on it we shall be only too delighted to do," said the gentleman, as the taxi which he had ordered came along, to take them to the hotel he had recommended as a quiet restful place, with a genuine old-fashioned Southern table known far and wide by travelers, and now being patronized by many air-minded tourists.

Perk had carried himself most commendably; this was easily done since he never once opened his mouth to say a single word, only grinned amiably whenever the courteous master of ceremonies said anything complimentary.

They were speedily booming along toward the adjacent city, with curious Perk bobbing his head this way and that, eager to see anything and everything that came in sight.

"Say, haow fine it seems to know yeou're onct again back in yeour native clime," Perk observed, talking rather loud, possibly for the chauffeur to catch, and then again because he was still a bit deaf, after so many hours with the clamor of a running airship ding-donging in his ears much of the time. "Talk 'bout yeour beautiful North, in my 'pinion it doant hold a candle to aour Sunny South, with its balmy air, the songs o' the mockin'-birds, the merry laughter o' the niggers, an' a thousand other things yeou never do forgit."

"Oh! you Dixie boys are all alike—nothing can ever wean you from your love for cotton fields, tobacco plantations, sugarcane brakes, and all such typical things of the South; but I like to hear you talk that way, Wally; it's in the blood, and can't be eradicated."

"Yes suh, that's what I reckon it shore is," and Perk relapsed into silence, possibly to ponder over that last word of Jack's, and try to get its true meaning.

He was soon deeply interested in what he saw, for Charleston is full of wonderful sights, to Northern eyes at least—fully on a par with quaint New Orleans, and Mobile—the iron lattices fronting many old-fashioned houses with double galleries—the churches that date back two hundred years at least, with their burial grounds filled with dingy looking stones and monuments, on which could be found chiseled numerous famous names of families connected with the history of this typical sub-tropical city—and occasional glimpses could be caught of that wonderful bay which is Charleston's pride and boast.

At the hotel they were speedily ensconced in a double room that boasted two beds—Jack usually looked to having things arranged that way when feasible, as Perk was a nervous sleeper, and apt to fling his arm across the face of any one alongside. It also afforded them a splendid view from the windows.

"I shore do hope, partner, you're reckonin' on aour havin' some fodder 'fore we tackle any business; 'case my tummy it's agrowlin' somethin' fierce; so I jest caint hold aout much longer an' feel peaceable—have a heart, buddy, fo' a guy what was born hungry, and gets thataway five times every day."

"That's all right, Perk," he was told, with a smile; "here are our bags, and we can fix up a bit, for I feel that a bath would do me a heap of good. Suppose we get busy, and by the time we look civilized again it will be twelve, which you remember the clerk told us was when the doors of the diningroom were thrown open."

"Gee! I only hope I kin hold aout till then," lamented poor Perk; "when I lamped the window display o' a boss restaurant while we come along I had a yen to jump aout, an' duck into the same, things looked so tantalizin' like."

"I can understand that yearning of yours, brother; but the sooner we get busy the quicker we'll be sitting down with our knees under a table, and ordering a full dinner for two. Go to it then, while I take a warm dip."

The agony ended eventually, and as it was then a quarter after twelve they decided to go down to the lobby, and partake of the fare which had been cracked up to them as especially fine, as well as indicative of typical Southern cooking—Perk kept harping on that same string until Jack whispered to him he must not overdo the matter.

Apparently they found everything to their liking, for they remained in the diningroom almost a full hour; and when they came out Perk was breathing unusually hard, like a person who has done heroic duty in an effort to show the hotel *chef* he appreciated his culinary arts.

"We'll take things easy in our room for a short while," Jack informed his chum, as they ascended by means of the "lift" or elevator. "Along about halfpast two I'll call up my friend, and distant relative, Mr.—er, oh! yes, Mr. Casper Herriott, and make some arrangement for joining him tonight at his home—I've always been a bit eager to see just what sort of family my—er second cousin Casper might have, and this will be an excellent opportunity to satisfy that—er *yen,* as you would say."

"Huh! jest so, suh, an' it shore pleases me to see how loyal yeou are to yeour illustrious fambly tree—second cousin is real good, I'd say, suh, mighty good connection."

"Take it all seriously, partner, even when we're snug in our own room—such things need constant *practice,* and shouldn't be thrown off and on just as the occasion arises; such a habit breeds carelessness, you must know."

"Jest so, suh, jest so; I takes the hint, okay," gurgled Perk.

CHAPTER XII

When Cousins Get in Touch

Jack was as good as his word.

At exactly half after two he was in touch with the office where the Government at Washington was ably represented by the gentleman he had been instructed to get in close intercourse with, unbeknown to outsiders.

"It this Mr. Herriott—Mr. Casper Herriott?" he asked, when he heard some one handling the receiver after the house operator had heard his polite request.

"It is," came back in firm tones.

"*Cousin* Casper Herriott?" continued Jack, a bit mischievously.

There came a slight exclamation, then—

"Who is it speaking, please?"

"Rodman Warrington, of New York, sir."

"Ah! just so, Mr. Warrington; I've been rather expecting to hear from you at any time. Glad you arrived safely; was that your ship I chanced to notice hovering over the airport about eleven?"

"That was the time we arrived, sir; to meet a warm welcome from your gentlemanly superintendent of the port. He saw to it that our craft was speedily placed in a hangar, where it can remain as long as we happen to be hunting along the coast. I presume, sir, the new amphibian is here, and waiting for me?"

"I'm delighted to assure you on that matter—it was brought here six days ago, and you will find it all safe and sound at the same airport where you landed."

"What arrangements have you made for my meeting you, er-Cousin Casper?" continued Jack.

Again he heard what he took to be a chuckle come over the wire, which assured him this Mr. Herriott at least was a man who appreciated humor, and seemed to be getting considerable enjoyment out of the happening, even though it was meant to all be along the line of strict business.

"You have my house address, I presume, cousin?" he thereupon asked.

"Certainly I have; it was you yourself sent it to me, sir, you remember." Jack went on to say.

"To be sure—that had quite escaped my memory, owing to a press of business for the Department. Suppose you come around, say at eight this evening, when I shall be delighted to see you."

"You can depend on me to be there; I have often wished I could drop in on you informally, and renew our old ties of friendship."

"Just so, and on my part I shall be most charmed to have you meet my good wife, and the children also, who have heard me speak of you more than a few times."

Both of them seemed to be enjoying this little chatter, meant to deceive any possible spy who might be looking for someone to make a business call upon the Government agent,—perhaps there might even be such a snake in his office force, some one who had been bought body and soul by the syndicate, which would account for a leakage more than once in the past, calculated to upset certain deeply laid schemes for breaking up the wide-flung conspiracy against Uncle Sam.

"I shall be particularly pleased to meet them, I assure you, cousin," continued Jack. "At eight you said, sir?"

"Yes, and while you are in the city, later on possibly, I'd like you to fetch around that splendid pilot chap you mentioned, I believe, in one of your letters,—let me see, I think you wrote he was a native of Birmingham, down in our own Alabama close by, a sort of an odd genius, in the bargain, to whom you had become greatly attached."

"I see you have been well posted, Cousin Casper," Jack told him, understanding of course how the gentleman must have had a duplicate of the code letter sent on to him, Jack; since they were to work in collusion as a team. "Yes, I shall try to coax him to come with me later on—you know he's not at all gunshy when in the field, or at the traps, a most excellent shot, and guide; but he doesn't take much stock in society functions, in which he differs somewhat from myself. I'll see you then tonight, cousin."

"We'll consider that settled; goodbye, Cousin Rodman until eight."

Jack was laughing as he switched off, as though this part of his mission might be looked upon in the light of a good joke rather than anything really serious. But no one knew better than Jack what lay behind this pretense—how it was to be taken as only a bluff in order to deceive any argus eyes, or hostile listening ears, that might be employed by the powerful syndicate to further the ends of the smugglers of the Carolina coastways.

When Perk heard what had passed he, too, had his little fit of merriment; but looked serious when Jack told him of the warm invitation received concerning his being brought to the home of Mr. Herriott some time later on.

"Shore, I'll be glad to go with yeou, partner," he affirmed, taking a big breath at the same time, as though he had succeeded in conquering his prejudice; " 'cause I wanter to meet up with this gent, an' hear what he's got to say. His lady, I done reckons, aint agoin'—agwyin' I means—to think much o' a ignorant guy like me; but if he's got *kids* why I'm allers at home 'long with them. Now tell me some more yeou two done talked 'bout."

"The real talking will come off tonight when we get in touch, Wally; all we did was to make arrangements; and whoever conceived this idea about our pretending to be distant cousins hit on a clever idea, and one that ought to throw any prowling spy off the track—whether in his office force, if they were listening to our little friendly chat, or even among the servants in his home."

Perk wanted to start out and see something of the city; and while Jack on his part would have preferred staying there, and going over his schedule of arrangements once more, he concluded it might be wiser for him to give in and accompany the other on his roving about the city; for truth to tell he still felt a little dubious about Perk's ability to play his part naturally at any and all times.

Accordingly they sallied forth, and securing a taxi had the driver take them to such points of interest as were within his ken. Perk was eager to see the noted navy yard, at some distance north of the city, but Jack convinced him that could very well keep for another time.

"At any rate, brother," he concluded, by stating, "you're going to look down on that same navy yard every time we take off on a flight of exploration, to learn whether the ducks are down from the Far North in sufficient numbers to tempt us sportsmen to locate, and build a duck blind."

"Gee! I kin see where I'm agoin' to enjoy a little shootin' fo' a change, suh," Perk went on to say, accompanying his words with one of his wide grins. "Aint done much practicin' on wild fowl fo' a heap o' moons, so I done reckon I'll show up kinder poor at fust; but it'll all come back soon's I gits my hand adoin' its cunnin', an' my eye on the job."

They were back in the hotel by sundown, with Perk trying to guess what he'd like best for his dinner.

"Wonder if so be they got any sorter dish I used to be fondest of when I was atrapsin' raoun' ole Birmin'ham as a gawky kid—somepin naow like stuffed possum with baked sweet yams—haow even the mention o' that lovely dish makes my mouth fair water, an' my eyes glisten like raindrops on the grass. Then there's co'nbread, hoecake we uster call hit in them days when—"

"Oh! you'll be sure to pick all your beloved dishes out of the menu, Brother Wally;" Jack interrupted to tell him; "only I hope you keep that appetite of yours in check; what would become of all my well-laid plans for a great kill of ducks and geese if I had to leave you on your back in a Charleston hospital here, down with gastro-enteritis, on account of an over indulgence in rich food?"

"Gosh amighty! doant mention that sort o' thing again, partner; I'll try an' bridle this ferocious appetite o' mine, an' hold her in check, shore I will. Gaster—trig—er whatever it was aint agwine to get a grip on *me*, no suh."

After dinner had been disposed of they again repaired to their room, Perk having an armful of papers with which he meant to pass the time while his chum was chatting with the Government agent, and picking up quantities of fresh information to add to what he had already accumulated.

Jack had him promise faithfully not to think of stepping out of the room, and to also refrain from opening the door to any caller.

"We're stacking up against a desperate bunch of dare-devils, don't forget, comrade, who'd hold life cheap—at least any other life but their own—if it had to be snuffed out in order to further their evil ends. In a case like this it's a whole lot better to overrate your enemy, than to think too cheaply of him. Have a pleasant time, and I'll be back inside of a few hours. So-long!"

CHAPTER XIII

Picking Up Facts

When Jack found himself shaking hands with his newly acquired "second cousin" one keen glance seemed quite enough to tell him Mr. Casper Herriott was a man after his own heart—genial, with a warm handclasp, yet possessing a firm jaw, a keen eye, and all the marks to signify that the Government had picked out the right type of business executive when he was placed in his present position of authority at the port of Charleston.

So, too, did he appreciate the delightful lady who gave him her hand and a wise smile, as though she considered it rather amusing to thus meet a relative of her husband who had bobbed up out of a clear sky, and seemed to be such a worth-while young fellow, just the kind any lady delights to have enter her home, and meet her children.

These latter were a boy of about ten and a delightful little miss of perhaps six or seven, so pretty that Jack could hardly take his eyes off her bewitching face. He decided that of course they could not have been taken into the secret, and actually believed him to belong to their father's family.

For some little time they sat and talked on general topics; the children presently going to bed as though their time had arrived; also expressing the wish that they would see the new relation again very soon—evidently Jack had made as favorable an impression on the youngsters as upon their parents.

Mrs. Herriott soon turned the conversation into aviation channels, as though realizing that certain information she had been desirous of obtaining along the line of the new fad might be furnished by this wide-awake young chap, who moreover, she had undoubtedly been told by her husband, was one of the brightest and most successful of the men of the Government Secret Service active roll.

Jack, being filled with knowledge pertaining to his life calling, the mastery of the air, took extreme pleasure in giving her explanations to her queries that apparently afforded the lady much satisfaction.

Then along about half-past eight Mr. Herriott made some plausible excuse for asking his guest to accompany him to his "den," where he wished to ask his professional opinion in connection with with a fine new hammerless Marlin repeating shotgun, which he had lately purchased, with the intention of later on spending a few days among the mallards and black ducks at a club he had joined.

It was indeed a fact that he had such a brand-new gun, which he handed to Jack, with a whimsical smile; the other carefully looked it over; tested the hammerless feature; saw that it was a six-shot twelve-bore Marlin shotgun, and then gravely handed it back with words of the highest praise, just as though he had been examining a new production of an old friend.

"I can well understand how you'll have considerable enjoyment out of that hard-shooting gun, sir," was his warm comment; "I've been out in a sneakbox with one of the same pattern, and found it trustworthy beyond description."

"I'll just lock the door so we may not be disturbed by some servant, and then we can have a heart-to-heart confab—Cousin Rodman!"

Both of them smiled in unison at the conceit; and then, having fixed the door to his satisfaction, Mr. Herriott drew his chair alongside the one into the depths of which Jack had sunk, following a wave of his host's hand in that direction.

"In the start let me acknowledge that I've been a bit keen about meeting you, Mr. Ralston," he went on to say, warmly; "I've heard certain matters discussed, as far as such are spoken of in our circles, and had conceived a very high opinion of your abilities along the line of the hazardous profession you are following. I chance to know at the same time how well they think of you up above; and that they have shown this by the fact of entrusting such a difficult task to your working out. I am in full sympathy with what you plan to attain, and shall do anything and everything in my power to assist you to a complete success."

"I am sure that is most kind of you, sir," Jack hastened to say; "and I hope to pick up many valuable points through my association with you, which is so fortunate; because there are still many things I should know better than I do, and which must be mastered before I can venture to make a real start in the game."

"It pleases me to hear you say that, since it shows how you appreciate the terrible difficulties, the overshadowing perils, and the enormity of the syndicate you will find yourself up against. It certainly requires a nervy chap to undertake to pit his wit and energies against so powerful a group as these men, of high and low degree, banded together for spoils only, have organized. And now, I presume you have a list of important questions which you wish to fire at me; so we had better be making a start."

All of this had been spoken in low tones, that could never have been caught beyond a closed door; besides, Mr. Herriott had cautioned his good wife to see that such servants as they employed in the house, all colored, and who were supposed to be absolutely reliable, were where they should be at that time of night, and not "snooping" about the halls, or outside near the windows, over which the shades had been drawn so carefully beforehand.

Accordingly, the way being now open for acquiring more or less information, Jack drew out a folded paper, and began to put the first question.

These things do not necessitate their being noted here, although to Jack they meant a great deal, serving to fasten in concrete form fragments of his view of the situation; and by degrees make a complete whole, thus giving him the grasp he required to accomplish his end.

Mr. Herriott answered slowly, as though anxious to make no mistake that might cost the bold workers unnecessary trouble or risk. He might have been a lawyer on the stand, so studiously did he tell whatever he happened to know of the point Jack was trying to have made clear.

Jack was wonderfully heartened—with such a clean spoken and well informed witness in the chair he could already see things were bound to speed along, and bring him much grist for the mill.

When in the end his list of queries was finished, Mr. Herriott hastened to assure him he stood ready to answer any others that might occur to his new-found friend later on; for Jack had already mentioned how he and Perk would "stay around," possibly for as long as ten days, or two weeks, there was so much to learn, such great need for him to investigate many regions in that wilderness of swamp and watercourses marking the northward shore line.

So far as he had gone in the matter, Jack felt much encouraged; although knowing full well by far the worst was yet to come. These preliminaries seemed only in the nature of skirmishes, with the fierce battle in prospect.

Mr. Herriott had told him many things having a distinct bearing on the great adventure; mention of which will be made later on, when Jack starts posting his chum.

This was only the first of several interviews he expected to hold with the accommodating Government representative, as step by step he climbed the heights, and reached the climax just before plunging into the fray, on the principle that it was his duty to "hew close to the line, let the chips fall where they willed."

It was after ten when Jack arrived at the hotel. Feeling particularly dry before ascending to their room, he satisfied his thirst by stepping into the convenient drugstore, and supping a cold cream soda. This was on the principle that if he knew Perk—and he had reason to believe he surely did —the other might be expected to shower him with questions of every variety, in his eagerness to learn how their plans were progressing; so that his throat would soon become too dry to keep up the chatter necessary to appease the voracious one.

He found Perk drowsing in his chair, the evening paper scattered all over the floor, as it had been tossed aside after being perused in search of such items along the line of aviation and Government work in suppressing lawless breaks in the customs service and coast patrol, always matters of supreme importance in the eyes of a loyal and industrious Secret Service man.

Perk jumped up when the door opened, as if suddenly realizing that after all he had neglected to fasten it as Jack had advised.

"By gum! if I didn't jest furget 'bout lockin' that door, partner!" Perk went on to exclaim, winking very hard as the electric light hit his eyes after his "bit of a nap;" but Jack said nothing in reproof, only settled down in a chair, beckoned the other to draw alongside, and calmly remarked:

"Got an earful for you, brother—lots of interesting things to tell; and you want to make a mental note of each and every one, so's not to forget if the occasion arises. Now listen, and be prepared to speak up if you're puzzled."

CHAPTER XIV

PERK GETS AN EARFUL

"Go to it, ole hoss; I'm all set!" was the way Perk announced the fact that every atom of drowsiness had fled from his eyes, and he was as wide-awake as any hawk that ever darted down on a farmer's chicken pen.

Accordingly Jack started in to tell of the pleasant time he had experienced while spending a couple of hours with Mr. Casper Herriott and his charming family.

Perk was mildly interested at first, which was saying a good deal, considering how anxious he felt to have the narrator "get down to brass tacks," as he himself would have expressed it; meaning facts intimately connected with the perils and anticipated progress of their present big adventure.

When, however, Jack reached the point where his host had made him promise to fetch his best pal along at some later date, as he was particularly anxious to meet and know him, Perk manifested fresh interest, and even asked several questions, thus learning what Mr. Herriott had said about having heard more or less concerning his, Perk's, good qualities—and eccentricities.

"Shore," he told Jack, soberly. "I'll be glad to meet up with the gent any time yeou see fit to invite me along—mebbe when yeou've sorter got matters hitched to the post, an' we're figgerin' on jumpin' off fo' keeps. I doant know 'baout the lady, since I aint much on talkin' to sech; but I'd jest *love* to see them kids—got a soft spot in my ole heart fo' awl boys an' gals, 'specially them that aint much—er soperfisticated—hanged if I know haow to git that ere word; but anyway yeou ketch my meanin', partner."

Then Jack began to branch off to other things, with Perk sitting there, his eyes never once leaving the face of his chum, drinking in every low-spoken word as though he meant to print the same indelibly on the tablets of his memory—a bit fickle, it must be confessed, when he was caught unawares.

One thing followed another, and the interest seemed to increase rather than diminish; until Perk was breathing hard, and making a whistling sound between his set teeth, a little habit he had when intensely excited.

"I asked about the amphibian that was to be placed at our disposal," Jack informed the other later on; "and Mr. Herriott apologized because, as he said, he understood it had been decided best and safest for all concerned if instead of the wonderful new navy speed boat, one of the latest patterns along that line, as first designed for us, they had sent a much used Curtiss Falcon; although certain new fangled devices had been attached, such as combination wheels and pontoons, that had been successfully tried out in active service, and were much the worse for wear, but staunch for all that."

"Gee whiz! that's goin' to tickle a feller named er-Wally a heap, let me tell yeou, buddy!" exclaimed Perk, with glistening eyes. "Allers did hanker to see haow that ere contraption panned aout. What else is there 'baout the boat we'll 'preciate, boss?"

"A number of up-to-date things that are apt to come in handy," Jack told him; "but remember, pains have been taken to make it appear they've been attached to the flying ship for quite some time—it might look suspicious if they were all *new*, as though placed there for some particular purpose—get the full meaning of that, do you, Wally?"

"Yeah, jest so," the other made answer, a bit hesitatingly, but with growing assurance in his manner; "them bally guys got sharp eyes, an' if so be they happens to have a spy right hyah in Charleston town, he'd lamp sech extravagance, an' keep an eye on weuns."

"That's the right answer, boy—you said it. Well, another fine thing Mr. Herriott told me, was connected with a suppression of the row made by our exhausts. You know that's been a source of great annoyance to us in times past, when it meant a whole lot if we could get close to our intended quarry without kicking up such a tremendous racket that every living thing inside ten miles must know an airship was somewhere around."

"Hot-diggetty-dig! air yeou tellin' me they done got that squall muzzled at last—that yeou kin make a grand sneak up on yeour meat withaout them suspectin' a single thing?"

"Well, they do say it's pretty close to having the noise kept under perfect control," Jack went on to state. "Whenever you want to stop the staccato sounds from publishing your coming to the entire country, ten miles in every direction, all you have to do is to press a button, and the muffler gets down to business automatically. Even the whirling sound of the propeller has been fairly quieted in the same way."

"Say, that shore is great news!" Perk exclaimed, enthusiastically; "an' I'll be near crazy to see haow she works, aput in practice."

"Just hold your horses until tomorrow, when we'll go out to the field and take our first flight in the old cabin Curtiss Falcon ship, to find how she handles. I never had the pleasure of piloting one of that type of ships, and so there'll be a heap for both of us to learn."

"Shucks! I done handled a amphib many a time, but that was years back, when they didn't near come up to the new kind; an' with all them contraptions attached in the bargain. It's agoin' to be high sport dodgin' 'raound over them swamps an' wild sections o' territory, duckin' daown to settle on some bayou, or mebbe a meanderin' river with a fierce current, sech as I read they got close to the Atlantic seaboard—bet yeour boots it is, partner."

"I reckon you're right there, buddy; but for the present we mustn't have much thought for amusing ourselves—everything we do should have a decided bearing on the carrying out of our game."

"Shore thing, boss," agreed Perk, not at all dismayed at having cold water thrown on his high hopes; "but if so yeou happens to git a good chance to knock over a brace o' fat mallards, in carryin' aout the duckin' part o' aour program, why, there aint any crime 'baout makin' a nice cookin' fire ashore, be they, and havin' real wild game fo' supper? We gotter eat to live, yeou knows, an' I'm right fond o' duck, when in camp."

Jack grinned, and shook his head, even though

smiling, as if he found his chum's specious argument unanswerable.

"We'll leave all that to the future, brother," he told Perk; "it isn't always advisable to cross a stream until you come to it."

Then he went on to reel off still more of the information passed along to him by his late host; and while many things he told may not have seemed as important in Perk's eyes as the two just mentioned, nevertheless he tried to pay strict attention, and asked numerous questions, to convince Jack he understood all he said.

"And before we take off for a spin," Jack added, as an after thought; "we must get all the raft of things aboard the amphibian we fetched here to use in our work. There will be other necessary stuff to pick up from time to time, as we advance along our road; for we've got to remember that once we make the grand getaway we'll not see the floodlights or boundary zones of Charleston aviation field again until we've won our game; or come back defeated, as others have done before us, men supposed to be as clever as they make them in our particular line."

"Then we got a big day afore us tomorrow, eh, what, partner?"

"Looks that way, buddy," Jack lost no time in saying; "and on that account I reckon now we'd better call a halt on this talkie, and hit the hay. For one I'm about as sleepy as they make 'em, and ready to crawl between the sheets, leaving tomorrow to look after itself."

"Meanin' to run up an' see the gov'nor tomorrow, any?" queried Perk, as he started to take off his shoes, and suppressing a big yawn while so doing.

"I made an arrangement to get over to his house tomorrow night, should I have further questions to put up to him," Jack admitted. "Then again there's always a chance of some later important news coming in from Headquarters, such as we ought to hear about without delay, since it could bring about some sort of change in our plan of campaign."

Perk grunted, as though he grasped the idea; but was really too tired himself to think of asking more solutions of the possible puzzles as yet bothering his brain.

With the coming of dawn they were both astir, for when on duty Perk could cut his sleeping portion in two, if it was deemed necessary; while Jack had ever been able to get along with a few hours recuperation each night.

They went down and enjoyed a fine breakfast, although Perk had to be warned again not to founder; since they had a strenuous day ahead, when he needed to be in the best possible condition. Consequently he had to deny himself a third helping of sausages and fried eggs; as well as a fourth plate of griddle cakes; dripping with fresh butter and Southern syrup. However, he "opined" he would be able to hold out until lunch time; for which he meant to be provided by securing some stuff at a bakery, together with hard-boiled eggs aplenty—trust an old campaigner with vast experience for looking after the "eats" when backed by an abundance of the "long green."

When they had laid out a program that covered everything for the day, they took a taxi, and ran out in style to the aviation field. Jack assumed the post of running things, as was his right, acting as a wealthy young sportsman, used to doing just about what he pleased, and "letting the world go hang!"

He had a little chat with his good friend of the previous day, and they learned that their other ship, the Curtiss-Falcon, was housed in the same Blevins Aircraft Corporation hangar that now sheltered their big Fokker tri-motored craft; which made things doubly comfortable, when they would start changing their possessions from one to the other.

Jack only waited until some call took the superintendent off, leaving them by themselves, when with Perk's help he commenced the job of making the transfer. This had been taken into consideration before they left San Diego, and later on in the Curtiss-Wright hangar at Candler Field, Atlanta; so that everything had been placed in a series of cartons, such as might be tossed overboard when their contents were disposed of—particularly in the case of edibles, and such perishable supplies.

These handy cartons would have prevented any one from knowing what they were stocking up with, and in such wise warded off possible suspicions that might have started a string of happenings none too pleasant to contemplate.

After this job was completed came the running of the antique Curtiss cabin amphibian out of its hangar, and settled in position for the coming take-off; with Perk all agrin, as if he anticipated a glorious cruise.

CHAPTER XV

THE TRIAL SPIN

Perk had closely examined a number of things about the amphibian in which they anticipated carrying out the gigantic task committed to their hands by the Chief at Headquarters; and whom they looked up to as worthy of their utmost respect as an organizer able to consider the utmost details. Most of his scrutiny, however, did not have any connection with new gadgets affixed to the black dashboard fronting the pilot's seat; but lay in the direction of the combination of wheels for landing on solid ground, also pontoons for use when seeking to drop down on the water of river, lagoon, or even the sea itself.

He spent considerable time in examining the working of this contrivance, which he had reason to fully appreciate—if only it proved all that was claimed for it, which was soon to be settled.

Then the new-fangled muffler for the engine exhaust was a source of vast attention on Perk's part; Jack could see him shaking his head incredulously; and from this suspected Perk of doubting its efficiency; but then Perk happened to be something of a skeptic, and even though he did not come from Missouri he usually had to be shown before yielding his doubts.

"Let's get out of here, and aloft," suggested Jack, when he found it was about an hour before noon time.

The field just then presented a rather animated appearance, as ships were coming in, and going out; with several taking up parties who were eager to try a first air swing. This just suited Jack, for it would keep many curious eyes off their movements; and just then the less notice they drew the better he would be pleased.

They picked up a couple of field workers to lend a hand, and hence their rather seedy looking water and air craft was wheeled into position, after it had been serviced while yet in the hangar, a very nice undertaking for one who disliked publicity.

"Here, Wally," Jack went on to say, when everything seemed in readiness for their initial jump, "suppose you take hold, seeing you're more accustomed to this type of boat than I am. However I'll soon get acquainted, and then it'll be okay. Step in, and grab the stick, partner; nothing to keep us on ground that I know of; and I'm anxious to have a look-in at the waterways where we're hoping for a run of luck with the ducks and geese."

Much of this of course was for the benefit of

the two men in dungarees, for how were Jack and his pard to know but that one of them might turn out to be a clever spy in the pay of the never sleeping Combine, jealous of their hitherto unsurpassed success in beating the customs, and in a way daring the Secret Service branch of the Federal Government to "do its level best to down them"?

Perk was not in the least averse to taking the place of honor when the amphibian would start its initial flight in their hands. He proved the absolute truth of what he had said about being fairly at home with the ship that belonged to both the land and water contingent; for they made only a short run when contact with the ground was cut off, and like a bird broken away from its brass cage and soaring upward, they started to spiral in the effort to gain altitude.

When he had a ceiling of say about five hundred feet or more, Perk commenced a wide swing, wishing to circle the city on the seashore, to view it from a different angle than their former experience had given them.

"Now point her blunt nose into the north, buddy —we're off!" Jack bawled in the ear of the pilot, the ear-phones not having as yet been adjusted— all those things came under the line of Perk's duty, and would be attended to in due time.

They speedily left the good city of Charleston

behind them, and were passing over the Navy-yard; which place Perk meant to examine more closely with his glasses on another occasion, when matters would be easier for him.

"How does she go?" shouted Jack, later on, when they could no longer catch even a fugitive glimpse of the city, saving the cloud of smoke that almost always hung over the high buildings and steeples.

"Bang up, boss; works like a charm!" yelled Perk, happily, as though he was not "caring a Continental" just how long Jack allowed him to hold the post of honor. "Whoever looked after the job o' gettin' this classic old-timer in great shape for this work, he shore knew his onions, I'll say. It's a snap to run this boat, if yeou want to know my 'pinion."

"I think I'll take a whirl at the controls, partner!" cried Jack; "stay just where you are for a while at least; I can play the game as a back-seat driver. Here goes, then."

He was pleased to find it no trouble whatever to handle the amphibian as though he knew everything about such craft; after all airships are run pretty much alike; and it depends on the adaptability of the pilot as to whether he can work the same as with his own familiar type of craft— there are some people who are able to master any and all models of automobiles, even though handling them for the first time, especially men mechanically inclined by Nature,—and Jack happened to belong to that class.

"You can go about your duties, Wally; I'll work over into the front seat okay, for its an easy job, I reckon. When we make up our minds to dip down and wet the pontoons in some body of water, fresh or salt, I'll let you handle the boat again; though I imagine I could do the thing without much splash if I was put to it. I'll soon get the hang of the trick, you can well believe."

"Huh! yeou would, Mister—it aint much that'd faize yeou, take it from me as knows."

After that conversation was such a tremendous effort that it languished until a better opportunity opened up—this would come when Jack found it expedient to make a test of the muffler system, with which their boat had been supplied, and which Perk was eager to see tried out.

To the delight of both fliers the device worked to a charm, most of the deafening racket being abated, even when they going at the fastest speed of which the "has-been" Curtiss-Falcon was capable of exhibiting—much more than a hundred miles an hour, Perk figured.

"Huh! mebbe naow they call this ship a relic o' the past," he grunted, when the success of the experiment was assured; "but I wanter say right naow there aint amany up-to-the-minute ships as kin run circles 'raound this *tub*, as some wise guy pilot'd call her. See, yeou kin hear ev'ry word I'm asayin' an' yet I aint ahollerin' any to notice. It's a bully invention, an' shows where we're agettin' in this science o' aviation. From what I hears, them ships as is acarryin' smuggled stuff 'long the seaboard aint great at speed, 'cause they don't need to be, their job bein' to carry hefty loads each trip, an' be steady goers. If the chanct ever comes to try this Falcon aout agin one o' that dirty bunch, I'm wagerin' we'll overhaul the same hands down, an' no takers."

"I hope your prediction proves a true one, brother," Jack told him; "for, come to think of it, there's a pretty good chance we may yet be up against a hot chase, either the pursued, or better still, the pursuer; in either case having the speediest craft would be an advantage worth while. Yes, that seems to be okay, and a big improvement over all that row we're accustomed to carrying along with us wherever we go."

They had been heading up the coast, keeping within sight of the Atlantic most of the time; but paying constant attention to inland pictures.

Or course Perk had before then brought his faithful and much beloved glasses out of their nook, and was making frequent use of the same, staring this way and that, sometimes making a noise with his mouth as though grunting his surprise to discover what a clear atmosphere attended their trial flight, and how close up the powerful binocular lens brought far distant objects.

"It shore is a big treat jest to be squattin' hyah, suh, an' observin' so much all 'raound us. Looks like a mighty tough region daown there, I got to admit; an' if them slick guys air ahidin' their landin' place where them awful swampy tracts lie, we're agoin' to have aour hands right full alocatin' the same, an' gettin' what we come after in the bargain."

"Don't worry, partner," Jack told him, in as smooth a voice as though he could see nothing whatever to cause undue anxiety. "Rome, you may remember, wasn't built in a day; there'll be heaps of time to get our little work in; and we were told to take as long as we thought wise—that there was no need of trying to wind things up in a hurry."

"That's correct, boss," admitted the easily convinced Perk; and then deftly turning the talk in another quarter he went on to add, pointing as he made the remark: "Looky yondah, suh, see that neat lit' bayou jest anestlin' there like a private pond. Wouldn't it be fine if we could on'y drop

daown, an' try aour pontoons on that sheet o'
water. Doant seem to be a livin' thing araoun'
neither, less it might be a 'gator, stickin' his nose
up to see if the coast it be clear."

Jack turned the craft to a severe dip, at which
the pleased Perk grinned horribly, as if he considered he had made a real "wise-crack."

"Goin' daown, folks—main floor next—ev'rybody aout then what aint agwine to the basement!"
he went on to remark, quaintly; and Jack could see
how his best pal was earnestly trying to acquire the
genuine Southern manner of speech, tinctured
with a touch of negro dialect.

"I'm going to try to make contact myself,
brother," announced the confident pilot, as, after
several circling movements he headed up against
the sea breeze that was blowing from the southeast just then.

Perk did not appear to feel any concern, such
confidence did he have in the other's ability to
make landings so soft that an egg would hardly
have been crushed by any jumpy motion.

Jack watched his contact with the water—the
big boat dipped, sprang up, came in touch again,
and then settled down to making headway, the little
wavelets curling away from the bows of the pontoons with a murmurous sound very similar to the
gurgling of a running mountain brook.
(155)

"Splendid work, buddy, better'n I could a done it myself, with all the sperience I done had long ago. An' she does work to a charm, sure as yeou're born. We're in bully great luck, all right, to have 'em pick aout sech a dandy ole boat like this, that does her makers credit, I'll tell the world."

Jack was not planning to stay in that lonely bayou for any length of time; what they were out to pay particular attention to on this their initial trip was the lay of the land; also to familiarize themselves with the working of the amphibian; so presently he again left the water, and arose like a lark.

CHAPTER XVI

ALL IN A DAY'S WORK

"And I gotter to admit," Perk was saying, shortly after they had gained the altitude that gave him a chance to sweep the horizon with his glasses, "even the ole weather sharp stands in aour favor. Look at that sky, buddy; did yeou ever in all yeour life set eyes on a clearer stretch—nary a single cloud pokin' its nose in sight; an' to think o' the measly days an' nights I uster spend in the mail-carrier business, asloggin' 'long with a capacity load, and mebbe ice formin' on my wings to beat the band. Yeah! this lay o' aourn aint so bad —some o' the time."

They swung over much of the territory for fifty miles north of Charleston, with Jack noting the lay of the land as cleverly as any topography expert charting a region, could display. In that wonderful brain of his he undoubtedly must have been engaged in making a mental chart of the ground; the sinuosities of the streams that ran with such eccentricity toward the nearby ocean; the numerous more or less possible landing-places where both boats from salt water, and those dropping

133

down from the clouds, might find a resting place; where their contraband cargoes could be taken aboard waiting trucks, and be transported to safe havens, despite the utmost vigilance of the customs officers and coast patrol forces to apprehend them.

This initial survey of the vast territory open to the expert smugglers, most of it absolutely familiar to those engaged in the illegal traffic, undoubtedly must have impressed the Secret Service man with the immensity of the task so recently placed upon his shoulders.

Just the same, the only visible result of this realization lay in a tightening of Jack's firm lips, and a fresh gleam in his steady eyes, as though he might be once again dedicating all his energies, his life itself, to the undertaking as yet so young, so untried.

"So much for the territory close to Charleston," he told his mate, as he turned the nose of his airship once more toward the city; "I've got that down pretty pat for a beginning. The next time we come out it will be to take up the survey about where we left off today, and head further north."

"Judgin' from what yeou say, partner, I kinder gu—reckons as haow yeou kim to the conclusion they gets their business in further away from dear ole Charleston—haow 'bout that, suh?"

"Possibly so, Wally, but from what I've

picked up from many sources, I'm already half convinced we'll be apt to run across the whole works within fifty miles or so of the city, it may be where that swift and crooked Yamasaw River skirts the coastways, dodging this way and that, even running backwards sometimes, so when you've been going with the current two hours you find yourself within a biscuit toss of a tree you passed long ago."

So in due time they dropped down again on the landing-field close to Charleston.

One thing Perk felt absolutely certain about, which was that his chief was not going to start real operations until he had accomplished the most exacting examination of the entire ground; and felt able to picture in his mind just how the Government baiters carried out their extensive smuggling game by sea and air; but when he *did* strike it would be in a way to start strangling the hitherto successful campaign of the giant Combine.

They both carried on in a perfectly natural fashion, much of their talk when in the company of any third party being along the line of their intended sport—how they had been able to discover a number of promising secluded ponds and bayous where already thus early in the ducking season a considerable gathering of the feathered game had been noted.

Perk fell into the humor of the trick, and even boasted of what a vacancy he meant to create in the flocks of ducks and geese before the termination of Mr. Warrington's vacation caused him to start north once more to his regular "business" of attending Board meetings in a bunch of companies where he chanced to be a heavy stockholder, and a director as well.

Really to Perk, who liked a joke as well as the next one, this thing promised no end of fun; every hour of the day found him more deeply interested than before, and eager to push ahead.

That night in the sanctity of their room, (speaking even there in low voices as if they more than half believed the very walls might have ears) Perk took occasion to mention the remarkable gift his companion had with regard to a retentive memory.

"I jest doant see haow yeou kin 'member things like yeou do, ole hoss," he was saying, evidently fishing for light on a subject that had often confounded his intellect. "Onct yeou hears a longwinded talk, an' I'll be hanged if yeou can't spin her off word fur word, an' never a single slip-up. Haow kin yeou do it, suh, I'd shore like to know?"

"It just can't be explained, brother, and that's a fact," Jack told him in his smiling way. "All you know is that Nature's been kind in giving you such

a faculty, and let it go at that. I may seem remarkable to you, in that I've got such a good
memory; but there have been others beside whom
I'm a regular piker. Did you ever hear of Blind
Tom, brother?"

"Huh! 'pears to me I did—he was some sorter
black man, wa'nt he, suh, what could play extra
good on the pianner?"

"Extra good—why, that doesn't mean a tenth
of what he could do—one of the greatest natural
phenomena ever known in America, or anywhere
—he was black as the ace of spades, and unusually
homely, so they hated to watch him when he was
playing; yet he had the most astounding memory
ever heard of—didn't know one note of music from
another—just depended on his ears, and that amazing talent that Nature had implanted in his
strange uncouth soul."

"What could he do, partner, as was so wonderful?" demanded Perk, seemingly more or less interested.

"Of course I never saw or listened to him play,
for he was dead long before my time," Jack continued; "but I've heard people who had, and I've
also read accounts of it in magazine articles, so
I'm pretty well posted myself. If you turned your
head away, they say you'd have sworn some famous composer was hitting the ivories of the piano,

and bringing out the most divine strains ever heard. He could listen just *once* to some classical and difficult sonata played by an eminent performer, (something Blind Tom had never heard before in all his life) and then sitting down he would reproduce the whole selection exactly as the famous artist had played it, with never a chord missing. People used to be awed, as though realizing they were in the presence of a miracle!"

"Gee whiz! it must a been somethin' fierce, Boss," was Perk's only comment.

"You know they say the Chinese and Japanese are wonderful imitators, and can reproduce any pattern to the minutest detail that is placed before them; but the best of them would be ten classes below that negro genius. So don't think I'm anything but a tyro, brother, with my poor memory.

"Hot-diggetty-dig! but yeou're good enough to make a poor bucko like me take a seat way back; that's the honest truth, er Mr. Warrington, suh."

As the following day broke with a promise of more clear weather Jack decided to waste no time. Accordingly they were off again, and speeding toward the north at a pace well over a hundred miles an hour.

"Gosh-a-mighty! I never'd have reckoned this here ole boat could hit it up so pretty," Perk at one time called out, when they had muffled the engine exhaust so effectually that they were well able to converse without raising their voices to a shout. "She muster been built outen A Number One stuff to hold together like she's done. If we got through this here job alive, partner, it's gwine to be up to us-uns to write a sweet letter to the company what constructed this here amphibian, an' tell 'em jest haow much we thinks o' aour boat."

"Possibly we may, partner," the other told him; "but even that might break the Secret Service rule of keeping identities well covered up, lest you lose some of your effectiveness by getting too familiar. Besides, I've got an idea this boat's been reconstructed—that as originally built she wasn't in the amphibian class at all—some gent who owned her must have been fond of the model, and feeling the necessity for having a ship that could land on water, had her altered to suit his wants."

"That may well be, suh," Perk went on to assert, with one of his nods; "but jest the same they made a mighty good job o' it, I'm asayin', suh. Huh! to tell the truth right naow I wouldn't cry much if I never did see aour ole bus, the big Fokker, agin; I've fell so turrible hard fo' this hyah ship, built to imitate a duck, what kin swim on the water, rise from the same when yeou wants to git agoin', an' cut ahead at more'n a hundred clean an hour. Huh!"

When they had reason to believe, (from landmarks taken notice of on the preceding day by Perk, as they turned for home) they were covering a fresh stretch of land and water, their vigilance was once more centered upon the task of closely observing every detail, and making more mental notes.

During this cruise they discovered next to nothing incriminating—as a rule they found themselves gazing down on a tangled mass of forest growth, with silver threads of water running crisscross here and there; or it might be muddy looking rivers and creeks meandering along in their long march to the sea, covering at least ten miles where a crow would fly the same distance in one mile or possibly less.

Jack had noted a number of places where the conditions seemed more or less favorable for such secret work as the successful landing of illicit cargoes necessitated; but while the spot seemed everything that could be wished, there was never a sign of its being used for such purposes—no sheds, or even a well-used road leading into the pine woods, such as must be required if heavy truck loads of goods were to be carried off.

"It looks as if we'll have to go over that first fifty or sixty miles again, with a fine tooth comb," Jack told his comrade, as the afternoon caught them still speeding gaily along, not over three thousand feet above the checkered landscape below.

"What we agoin' to do 'baout hit, then, suh?" demanded the puzzled Perk. "We shore caint keep startin' aout from Charleston every mawnin' like we're adoin' right naow, covering hundreds o' miles, an' hope to git back by daylight."

"Oh! that needn't trouble us anything to speak of, matey," the other hastened to assure him. "If necessary we'll drop down, and make camp for the night, pick things up in the morning, and take chances of getting back to Charleston any old time later on."

"Say, less do that same tonight, suh," suggested the artful Perk, with his most engaging smile; but Jack shook his head in the negative.

"Possibly we may tomorrow; but I've agreed to see Mr. Herriott tonight, partner."

CHAPTER XVII

Spinning the Net

Again, after Jack had paid a visit to the home of Mr. Herriott he repeated much of what fresh information he had picked up during the evening, some of which he deemed more or less important, as the facts dove-tailed with other details, to make something of a complete structure.

"Tomorrow we'll hang around the city, as there are a few things I've got down on my list of wanted articles," he observed in conclusion. "Besides, I promised him I'd fetch you around so as to make his acquaintance, for he always asks about you."

"Huh! Spose I jest *has* to get over there some time'r other," Perk remarked, as though not particularly eager to go. "But I shore hopes as heow on the follerin' mawnin' we kin start off, an' go so far we'll jest *have* to make camp in them there dark gloomy lookin' pine woods."

"It must depend a whole lot on the kind of weather they dish up for that day," Jack informed him. "It it's foggy, and the visibility poor, we might as well hang out here in the city, since we

couldn't do any paying business looking into a
blank wall of fog, you know, Wally boy."

"Okay—suits me jest as well as things go," the
other announced carelessly enough; "I aint acarin'
a scrap whether school keeps or not, so long as we
gits aour three square meals a day, an' dandy ones
at that, real Southern style, like I used to have
when I was a Birmin'ham kid, runnin' raound
barefoot with my mates, jest like Tom Sawyer
an' Huck Finn uster do in them ole Mississippi
days we done reads 'baout in the books."

It was just as well that Jack had decided to drop
a day in their search for hidden haunts of the
smugglers; for when morning came the sky was
overcast, and poor visibility seemed to be "on tap"
for the entire day.

Jack went about doing his errands, while Perk
seemed content to stick to the isolation of their
comfortable room, doing some reading of the
bundle of well known daily papers he had managed
to secure at a shop they passed during the short
walk taken in company after breakfast—that, and
the waiting to get up an appetite for dinner seemed
to be the full extent of Perk's ambition, it was
plain to be seen—when he had a day off, and the
"eats" were so unusually tempting, it pleased Perk
to act as if a lazy streak had gripped him.

"I think I forgot to tell you," Jack chanced to

tell his comrade as the afternoon began to wane, "that we are invited to dine with Mr. Herriott and his fine little family tonight. Oh! you needn't be so alarmed, partner; we'll simply clean up, and look a bit dressy; you'll soon be on good terms with both him and his charming wife; as to the kids I warrant you fall dead for them at first sight."

Perk, whose face had at first taken on an expression of sheer dejection, seemed to brighten up at mention of the youngsters; for he even grinned, and started to the bathroom, as if to begin washing up.

They arrived in good time, and Perk was soon made acquainted with the entire little family—of course under the name and character beneath which he was hiding his own identity at that particular time.

Just as sagacious Jack had surmised would happen, Perk was soon feeling quite at home, making "wise-cracks" with the two wideawake youngsters, and even engaging in more or less conversation with his host and Mrs. Herriott.

It chanced that there seemed to be a dearth of news that evening, so they could spend the time after dinner in other ways than "going into a huddle," as Perk put it, and having a siege of explanations and surmises.

Mr. Herriott coaxed Perk to speak of his early

experiences, partly when over in France, during
war times, then later on with the Mounted Police
up in Northwest Canada, and also as one of the
early pilots carrying the mails, as far as was done
in those bygone days and nights.

When Perk was once fairly aroused he apparently lost his customary bashfulness, and could tell
a story that brought out more than a few laughs
because of what queer things he narrated, and his
comical way of relating the same, his expressive
freckled face all working with imitations of how
other men did their talking.

"I never sits so comfy in the cabin o' a up-to-
date tri-motored airship these here days," he went
on to remark, when well started, "with all sorts o'
instruments to navigate by, that I doant think
'baout heow we don't fly any more by jest instinct,
like we uster do when the Wright boys was a per-
fectin' their fust crude heavier'n air flyin' ship. Today, suh, we sits at the controls, an' keeps aour
eyes on aour instruments all the time, an' doan't
care a red cent what aour wonderful *instincts* say
'baout it."

"I never thought about that fact, Wally," Mr.
Herriott hastened to exclaim; "please go on, and
tell us something more along that same line. You
certainly must have passed through some strange
experiences, I'd say."

"Shucks! but it shore does make me laugh aout loud when I looks back to them early days, an' 'members the funny way we used to find aout whether the silly bus was a movin' up, er daown, to the left, or to the right. The very fust instrument, if yeou could call it that, to ease up on the instinct way o' doin' was invented by one o' them smart Wright brothers. Say, it was on'y a light piece o' string, tied jest in front o' the pilot's face. When we was a goin' near ten miles an hour, mebbe fifteen at a stretch, we kept an eye on that string right along, an' could tell what the ole ship was adoin', 'cause like it might a been if she floated in the wind straight at aour face we knowed we was keepin' on a level keel—if it went daown a bit why we was climbin' some; if the string struck us in the forehead in course the plane must be droppin'; and same way if it flowed to the right, or the left. An' say, I never did know that early Wright invention to kick over the traces, an' fool me any."

Even Jack apparently had never heard about that clever device, however primitive it might seem when placed alongside the wonderful means at present used to ascertain the same things—such as slipping, skidding, turning, climbing, or diving —today the experienced pilot watches the air-speed instrument, his compass, the bank and turn indicator. Only by placing entire dependence on the instruments in the cockpit can a pilot fly with any certainty in foggy weather, when it is utterly impossible to see any fixed point, either on the earth below or in the heavens above.

And this is only one great change made in both the construction of the airship in these modern days, as well as the helping hand given the pilot through the clever devices by which he is confronted when sitting at the controls.

Taken in all Perk spent a very pleasant evening with the Herriotts, and on their part they had a most uproarious time, the children particularly in romping with the jolly chap from the North.

It was with considerable eagerness that Perk bounded out of bed on the ensuing morning, and rushed to a window to ascertain what the chances were for a promising day in the coast skyways.

"Okay, partner!" he sang out blithely, after one brief look at the heavens, a portion of which was visible from the hotel window; "agwine to be jest fine, an' never a whiff o' fog aout there on Charleston harbor an' bay."

"Then we'll get busy, and make as early a start as possible," Jack announced, also quitting his cot.

"An' we doant kim back thisaway tonight, either, I shore reckons, Boss," Perk went on to add, with a happy ring in his voice; for he did yearn to eat one camp meal, when the chance came along, and no harm might follow their change of a set programme.

"That depends on a good many things," Jack warned him; "so I wouldn't count too heavily on our stick-it-out idea, if I were you, Wally, boy. If all goes well, no accidents happen to our boat, and we get so far away from home along about the middle of the afternoon, why we'll decide then on our doings for the night. You might as well, I suppose, carry a few necessary things along, such as you'd like to eat at a campfire supper—if we think it wise to have any fire, I mean."

"Oh! please doant throw any gloom on aour trip today, partnei; we kin make shore to drop daown in a region where there aint a Chinaman's chanct o' a solitary Tarheel bein' inside o' ten miles; an' the swamps araoun' makin' it ab-so-lutely impossible fo' sech to git to aour camp short o' six days anyway, havin' to cut his path through dense thickets; wade sloughs where the pizen water moccasins air thicker'n molasses on a cold mawnin'; with twelve-foot 'gators alayin' in wait to bite off a gink's leg quicker'n yeou could wink an eye. Shucks! we jest gotter have that same camp-fire—withaout the same it'd be like the play o' Hanblett with him left aout."

Jack only grinned, but Perk seeing the look on his face, took courage.

"There's one thing I haven't touched on as yet, brother, which might just as well be taken up now." Jack was telling his comrade, as they sat eating an early breakfast, there being hardly any one besides themselves in the diningroom; so they could talk in low tones, and keeping an eye on the waiters, so as to change the subject should one of them draw near.

"Huh! somethin' mebbe naow Mr. H been atellin' you-all, eh, suh?"

"Just that, Wally; but a matter of the utmost importance, it happens, as you'll soon understand, buddy. It concerns a certain party who's going to have a hand with us in closing the net, and making a big dent in this same syndicate we're up against. His name—bend a bit closer to me—is Jethro Hicks."

"Sho! never heard it afore, give yeou my affidavy, partner!" returned Perk.

"Of course not," snapped Jack; "neither did I until Mr. Herriott mentioned the fact last night that he would be waiting whenever we sent out the word—waiting in a certain little bayou which we'd have picked for our hideout—waiting in an old battered powerboat he owns, to take us about in the nest of swamps which we could never navigate otherwise. You get the point, don't you, Wally, boy?"

"Hot-diggetty-dig! jest what I do, suh; queer I never reckoned on haow we'd be able to dodge 'raound in sech crazy places, if left to aourselves. Gwine to have a reg'lar pilot—woods guide fo' swamp flittin', I'd call the same! Good enough, I say—caint be too many quirks set up fo' knockin' them dead game sports silly, to please me. As it is we gotter to be workin' with four hands each, if we hopes to climb 'em fo' keeps."

"I'll tell you more about this same Jethro Hicks when I get further word through our good friend, who's as interested in the success of our deal as we are ourselves—says he has it on his mind sleeping and waking, which pleases me a whole lot. Come, let's be on the move, partner; the chariot awaits us."

"Then we'll git aboard an' start right away, after I've laid in a few provisions that may keep the hungry wolf from aour door this very night. Let's go!"

Half an hour afterward and they were on their way out to the aviation field in a convenient taxi; where in short order their big amphibian, properly serviced by the field force, was ready for the take-off.

CHAPTER XVIII

BLACK WATER BAYOU

Fortune favored them again, it seemed, not only with regard to the skies, but, probably owing in part to the early hour, there were few persons scattered about the aviation grounds when they took off; and the regular attendants already understood the pair constituted a duck-hunting party, viewing the coast shooting stands with a view to getting in some good sport when finally satisfied as to location.

From the beginning they hit up a high pace, fully equal to the best the amphibian had thus far accomplished. Being what might be called "ambidextrous"—doubly able to leave by means of water, or solid land, it had not been necessary for them to locate on any river or bay, where they would not have the benefit of field mechanicians, and a movable filling station, as well as shelter in a comfortable hangar.

Jack had doubtless taken all such matters into consideration when forming his plans, and decided that the good points about staying at the regulation aviation headquarters outweighed the poor ones.

They covered the first fifty miles in short order, keeping at some distance further from the sea than on their previous trips, Jack having a new hunch, to the effect that possibly the rendezvous of the smugglers after all might be situated deeper inland than he had first suspected.

When later on Perk announced that he could just make out some city far off on the right, Jack pronounced it to undoubtedly be Georgetown, which lay at the junction of the Pedee and the Little Pedee.

They had flown directly over the same city on their previous trip, showing how far west of their original course they were now working.

"We're going to patrol this region most carefully, partner," Jack told his best pal, who as usual was handling the binoculars to the best advantage, and calling out any discovery worth while, so as to keep his mate posted. "It has all the earmarks to make it a dandy hidingplace, where these sinister operations could be pulled off, day or night, and no one the wiser. What easier than for a sea-going plane to swoop over or around Georgetown, coming from some unknown point east, and then vanishing in the distance, still going west? Get that, don't you, Wally?"

"Sounds all to the good with me, suh," the other told him, nodding as he spoke. "I'm atryin' to make aout some queer things daown there; but it's all sech a scramble I jest caint do much. Mebbe if we dropped a bit things'd seem different like."

"I'm going further west, so as to cover the ground," Jack informed him, as though his immediate plans were made up, and he did not care to change; "but later on in the day I reckon we'll be back this way, and possibly make camp for the night. I'd like to find out what sort of doings are taking place nights in this section; chances are we'll pick up some interesting points before striking Charleston again."

"Which same'd please me a heap, Mister," quoth Perk; who was by now beginning to grow a little weary of what he termed "inaction;" and sighing for more strenuous times to come along, when there would be some real thrills experienced.

At noon they partook of a "snack," devouring a few sandwiches, so as to take off the sharp edge of their appetites; Perk apologizing to himself for eating so scantily.

"If so be we're agwine to dine ashore alongside a gen-u-ine campfire," he went on in his whimsical fashion, "I wanter be in prime condition to do justice to the grub I'm meanin' to sling up fo' jest two gents, known to weuns as Mr. Rodman Warrington, an' er—Wally Corkendall, of Birmin'-ham, suh. So take things easy, an' jest forget haow yeou're still hungry, ole man; it's on'y what that lecturer says is a figment o' the imagination, an' so you're not a bit half starved."

When about the middle of the afternoon they again arrived in the neighborhood of the sector which had appealed to them both as well worth paying particular attention to, Jack signified that he was meaning to do something in the line of lowering their ceiling, and finding out whether there was a chance of their making a successful drop upon the waters of that queer bayou, alongside of which ran a swift and mysterious looking river he figured might be the Waccamaw.

Closer scrutiny convinced both of them that so far as their settling down on the surface of the lonely bayou was concerned, nothing could be seen that would interfere with such an arrangement.

Jack circled the spot several times, with his exhaust muffled, and even the propeller keeping unusually quiet, as though in full sympathy with their desire for secrecy.

"Cover every rod of both land and water with your glass, partner," he told Perk; "because it means a whole lot to us to make sure that there isn't any chance for hostile eyes to take note of our stopping here. Unless I'm away off in my reckoning this same bayou must be the identical place where we are to later on make a rendezvous with that cracker guide, Jethro Hicks, who knows every foot of these water trails—I understood he hid out in this terrible region for several years when at loggerheads with the authorities, though innocent of any crime. How does the ground look to you, buddy?"

"Like the ole Sam Patch, an' that aint no lie either, Boss," Perk lost no time in telling his mate; "I never did see sech a awful stretch o' mixed land an' water nohaow, nowhere; but jest the same that's zactly what we want, so's to make dead sartin they beant nobody araound hyah calc'lated to bother weuns, that's the way I looks at hit, suh."

"Quite right too, Wally, boy!" snapped Jack; "and such being the case here goes to settle down on that Black Water Bayou—I think that was the name Mr. Herriott gave the slough."

"Gosh all hemlock! an' it couldn't have a better name, I'm asayin' suh—tough enough lookin' to give anybody a shiver; but as we're itchin' fo' to keep aour comin' secret, it suits aour case to the dot."

There was plenty of room in the middle of the mysterious little lagoon for their landing, if such it could be called; and so cleverly did the pilot bring the pontoons of his craft in contact with the surface that hardly the slightest splash followed.

Jack lost no time in taxiing over to a certain spot that seemed to hold possibilities for the maneuvre he intended putting into effect—thick trees hung low over the water, and if only they could manage to push far enough in, the boat would be beautifully camouflaged—hidden under a fringe of branches, and so well disguised as to be discovered only after a close search.

"Wonderfully fine," was Jack's announcement after this had been successfully brought about. "Why, it's almost like late evening under this thick canopy; and the bayou itself, surrounded as it is with tall cypress trees, with those long trailing beards of gray Spanish moss give it a gruesome look."

"Urr! jest makes me think o' the ole graveyard I used to run past a goin' home late nights, when I was a country kid up in New England," Perk was saying, toning his voice down to almost a whisper.

It certainly did have a most funereal appearance, with the breeze making all manner of weird sounds through the tops of the trees, and the festoons of dangling moss waving to and fro like mourning banners; some unseen swamp creatures added to the shivering feeling that had attacted Perk by emitting the most gruesome grunts and groans his ears had ever heard.

"But it happens to be just what we were hoping to find," Jack continued, looking quite pleased at the loneliness of the spot; "small chance of any of those crackers coming in this direction, when they have no business here. I reckon Wally, you'll be able to have that jolly campfire your heart's so set on, without its getting us into any trouble."

"Huh! that all tickles me right smart, Boss," chuckled the other, rapidly conquering that sensation bordering on awe, and beginning to look at things in a more sensible light. "Kinder gu—reckons as haow there might be mebbe a 'gator or so in sech a slimy place as this same—that is, if sech critters do live as fur north as this South Carolina swampy region; anyhaow I ain't agwine to take chances awadin' in them nasty waters, where I kin see snakes aswimmin', and pokin' their heads aout to larn what in Sam Hill done drapped daown in their private park. Gee whiz! this is 'baout as cheerful a hole as the gateway to the Lower Regions, if yeou asked me what I thought, suh."

They soon discovered that they were not to be allowed to take things as easy as Perk may have anticipated; for presently both were employed shooing swarms of voracious mosquitoes from their exposed faces and hands.

CHAPTER XIX

THE LONELY CAMP

"Perhaps," suggested Jack, tiring of this exercise after a while, "it might be just as well for us to step ashore, so you can get that fire going. A little smoke would be worth while as a smudge to drive these skeets away; they're bent on eating us alive, it seems to me."

"Jest as yeou sez, Mister," Perk acquiesced, with alacrity; and in less than three minutes he had managed to jump ashore from the end of the wing that rested on a log close to the bank of the bayou.

Gathering some loose wood he quickly had a blaze going, and was joined by his comrade, who took particular pains to stand to leeward of the fire, so that clouds of thick smoke would cause the fierce insects to abandon the vicinity.

"I suppose that, generally speaking," Jack went on to say, "we would be hunting dry wood so as to send up as little smoke as possible, for fear of attracting notice, and bringing unwelcome visitors to our camp; but in this case the chance of detection plays a very small part in the game. We certainly need lots of pungent smoke in order to drive these hordes of nippers away. So go to it, partner, the more the merrier."

Later on they sat down where the wind would waft some of the smoke in their direction, and being at peace with the world just then found that they could compare notes, and reach certain conclusions.

Although the sun was still quite some little distance above the horizon, as they figured, (being unable to see anything through that mass of cypress, and hanging moss) it was already commencing to grow dusk back of the camouflaged airship.

"I knows as haow it aint time yet," Perk finally spoke up, getting to his feet with determination written large upon his face; "but jest the same I caint hold aout any longer—I got to listen to the growlin' daown below-stairs, as sez its past time to stoke the furnace; so sech bein' the case I'm ameanin' to start aour supper, if so be yeou aint no 'jections, suh."

"Not in the slightest, Wally, so get busy as soon as you like," he was told.

The other did not wait for a second invitation, but making his way back to the cabin of the amphibian presently returned with both arms full of mysterious packages. After depositing the same upon the ground near the blazing fire, Perk made a second trip aboard, and from that time on busied himself in the one occupation of which he seemed never to tire—making preparations to supply a rousing meal, cooked over such a bed of red embers as he delighted to supply.

Jack was pretty hungry himself, and enjoyed the spread greatly—its memory was likely to long haunt them; and in speaking of the past the time was apt to be set by such phrases as "something like a month after we had that glorious camp supper on Black Water Bayou, remember, partner?"

Jack sat there working at his maps for some time after they had finished eating; so, too, he made numerous notes, to be conned over and over again, until he could repeat the gist of them all as occasion arose. That was his way of preparing for a campaign; and no masterly tactics of a successful war general could have been an improvement on his programme—to prepare in advance for all manner of possibilities was as natural to Jack Ralston as it was to breathe; which plan certainly had much to do with the customary success falling to his lot.

Suddenly both of them caught the distant report of a gunshot; and stared at each other, as though mentally figuring what such a thing might signify.

"Did you take notice which direction that gunshot seemed to come from, eh, Wally?" demanded

Jack, presently, as no other similar sound followed.

"I'd say from over there," Perk swiftly replied, pointing toward the south as he spoke. "What dye reckons, suh, it'd mean?" he asked in turn.

"Oh! nothing that concerns us, I imagine, Wally, boy—some chap might have run across a hunting wildcat most likely, and couldn't resist giving him the works. But it settles the direction where that secret landing place may lie, I feel almost certain. That's one of the points I wanted to pick up; and before the night is over we may be able to prove my prediction sound."

"Yeou doant reckons, suh, they kin see this heah fire aburnin', do yeou?"

Jack laughed as though the idea had no standing with him.

"Not in a thousand years, Wally; it must be a matter of a mile, perhaps twice that between this spot and from where that gun was fired; you see, the night air heads toward us, and would carry the sound quite a long way."

He proved that he felt no uneasiness by continuing the conversation that had been interrupted by the sudden far-off shot; and so Perk did not hesitate to toss more fuel on his cheery campfire.

They were thinking of turning in aboard the nearby boat, and seeking their necessary rest, when Perk, who had unusually keen hearing, sat up and inclined his head to one side as though listening.

"Jest what she is, for a fack, partner," he went on to state; "an' shore as yeou're born, suh, they aint no muffler aboard *that* ship, I'll take my affidavy on that same."

"It *is* a ship, no doubt about that, and heading this way out of the east, you want to notice, buddy," Jack indicated, as though that mere fact had a deep significance in his eyes.

"Yeah! that's so," agreed Perk, readily falling in with the conceit, as he usually did when Jack was the originator of any proposition. "They air acomin' straight from aout on the ocean, where mebbe a steamer is alyin' anchored, an' loadin' its cargo o' contraband on fast blockade runners that come 'longside; also sky-carriers in the bargain, sech as drop daown close by on the sea, an' take on all they kin carry."

The faint sounds rapidly increased in vigor until even a novice could have decided it was an airplane making almost directly toward their strange camp on Black Water Bayou.

"Keep on listening, brother," advised Jack; "and then we'll compare notes as to where we heard the last clatter. Things couldn't be working more smoothly to suit our plans; and we ought to be pretty well primed by the time we come back here to join up with Friend Jethro."

Finally the now loud clatter ceased, which those airmen knew full well meant it had succeeded in effecting an apparently safe landing, whether on land or water they could only surmise.

So carefully had they both tried to get the exact locality fixed in their minds that when they came to comparing ideas it was found they agreed almost to a dot; so Jack was able by referring to his small compass to make a note of the circumstance, as well as their united conviction.

"I kin shut me eyes an' see what a busy bunch is workin' unloadin' that same crate," Perk observed, a little later on. "Scent's agettin' a little warmer, seems like, partner, when we ketch the racket o' a smuggler plane comin' in from the mother vessel away off shore, beyond the twenty mile danger line."

"I'd say it surely was," agreed Jack, grinning happily, as if in answer to the joyous look he detected on his partner's sunbaked face.

All had by now become as silent as the grave, at least so far as suspicious sounds undoubtedly caused by human agencies; but otherwise things did not happen to be so quiet. From the nearby swamp came a multitude of queer croakings and gurglings, accompanied by harsh cries such as night herons seeking their food, or other birds of similar activities, might make while fishing.

(155)

"Gee whiz!" Perk at one time burst forth, "did yeou ever in all yeour life listen to sech queer sounds as them? Hark to that splash—sure reckons some roostin' bird must a fallen off its perch, an' if all that flutterin' and squawkin' stands fo' anythin' its got swallowed up in the jaws o' some critter waitin' daown below fo' its supper. Glory! I wonder if weuns kin get any sleep with all these heah carryin's on in full blast. Jest hear 'em whoopin' it up, will yeou, suh?"

However, when the time did come for them to go aboard the boat and seek their cots, by closing the cabin door much of the noise was deadened, and after all Perk found little difficulty in getting to sleep.

Nothing occurred during the night to disturb them, or cause any undue alarm. Doubtless that variagated noise kept up through the livelong period of darkness, but it gave them no concern whatever.

When Perk happened to wake up he believed he could catch a feeble gleam as of daylight outside the cabin; and upon investigating found it to be a fact. He thereupon aroused his companion, and another fine meal was soon in process of preparation over a resurrected fire; to which of course the pair did ample justice, after which they made ready for another flight, and a return to the city.

CHAPTER XX

THE MOTHER SHIP

When Jack went over to the home of the affable Mr. Herriott the following night he had much to tell that gentleman, such as had a bearing on his own campaign. The other heard what he had to say, and then asked a number of pertinent questions that in their way were more or less helpful.

"From all you saw and heard, my friend," the other observed later on; "I am absolutely certain you have found a bonanza, and discovered the landing place used mostly by the planes that are carrying such vast quantities of contraband from mother ships to certain central depots, where doubtless motor trucks are able to come over unknown country shell roads, and convey the same to shore cities, possibly even as far north as Baltimore and Washington. You are getting close to your objective, I have no hesitation in saying; I only hope it all turns out as well and profitably as your daring and skill would warrant."

Such words from one whom he had come to admire as a "clean shooter," as Perk designated their official friend, gave Jack much satisfaction.

"Still, there's no reason for undue haste, you know, sir," he told the other in his calm way. "While I do not want to loaf on the job, at the same time I am against trying to push things to a decision, if by so doing I must take unnecessary chances."

"Quite right, too, Mr. er, Warrington," he was told. "It would have been much better for several of your fellows who worked on this affair if they had possessed a share of your caution; two in particular showed signs of getting somewhere but in seeking to make a swoop before the time was fully ripe they queered the whole game, and fell down on the job. I would be willing to prophesy that such will not be the result of your planning."

"There was one subject about which I'd be glad to hear something further, Mr. Herriott," Jack went on to mention.

"You have only to let me know what it is, and any knowledge I happen to possess in regard to the matter is at your service. Now tell me how I can give you any further assistance,—Jack."

"It's about that cracker guide who's agreed to take us to the secret landing-place of the mob— Jethro Hicks. Do you feel the utmost confidence in his honesty, sir? You can easily understand why I ask, since if it turned out that he himself was in the hire of this gang of law-breakers, things would turn out badly for myself and my friend."

"Let me reassure you on that score then," came the immediate answer; "I am positively certain Jethro will be found as true as steel. I know this from a number of reasons. First of all, I've been acquainted with the man for some years now, and I think I'm safe in saying that he thinks considerable of me as a staunch friend. I had an opportunity once upon a time, to do him a favor, when it seemed as though the whole world had turned against him, and kept him a fugitive from the law, hiding in the swamps and backwoods for some years; and he will never forget the little I was able to do for his family then. That is one reason why he has so greedily taken me up when I asked him to work hand in glove with you."

"Yet you say he had broken the law—was hiding from arrest apparently—hardly a fact to commend him as an honest man, sir, I'd think."

"But Jethro was entirely innocent in that nasty affair, as was later on proven without a doubt; he is now walking openly, and without a fear of arrest. On that same fact hangs his chief desire to help you break up this powerful gang of smugglers infesting the seaboard of our State."

"How come, Mr. Herriott?" questioned the surprised as well as deeply interested Jack.

"Listen, and you will, I am sure, understand

what I mean," continued the other. "Some years ago there was a sort of mountain vendetta existing between the Hicks family and two other households in the same neighborhood. It had gone on for a good many years, with occasional outbursts, and some shooting. Later on it came about that one particular man named Haddock made considerable money since prohibition came in; and still hating the name of Hicks found an opportunity to accuse Jethro of certain things, building up false evidence on which the young head of a family would undoubtedly have been sent to the pen if he had not hidden out in the swamps. While there this rich man also persecuted his family, and protected by his money could do this without hindrance.

"Jethro has never forgotten or forgiven those wrongs; and yet unlike many of his class, he does not wish to shoot his hated enemy down in cold blood. But it is more than suspected that John Haddock is one of the rich men backing up this big syndicate, for it would come directly in line with the way he managed to accumulate his own fortune in a less extensive way, merely with mountain dew as his stock in trade.

"Jethro swore to me he knew this to be a *fact,* although he could hardly hope to prove the same unless given an opportunity to raid their headquarters and find positive evidence there.

"Now you will understand just why he can be depended on—Jethro is no law-breaker, and his fierce hatred for John Haddock—all the Haddock tribe in fact—will make him a faithful assistant for such as you. Are you satisfied now, Jack?"

"Unquestionably so, sir; and I thank you very much for telling me this. I'll have a better opinion of Jethro, and feel a sympathy for him in his desire to get even with this rich schemer through whom he has suffered so much."

More of this confidential talk was indulged in, with Jack fortifying such conclusions as he had already reached.

And when he got back to the hotel room, to find Perk sitting up, reading, but eager to know if anything worth while had happened, he proceeded to further astonish his best pal by giving a verbatim rendering of every item spoken by the United States representative.

"So you see, brother, how well we are progressing," he concluded by saying; "and with such an eager helper as this same Jethro promises to prove, it looks as if something unexpected was going to strike that powerful illegal combine of smugglers at an early date—don't you feel that way too?"

"Shore I do, partner, an' here's hopin' it aint a-goin' to be so very long naow 'fore we get in aour fust crack. I'm near wild to knock one o' them smugglers' first aid ships to smithereens, with a nice baby bomb I got hid away aboard aour dandy amphibian cruiser."

"Your hour will strike in due time, Wally, boy," said the amused Jack, with a fond look at the excited face of his chum. "You've never completely gotten over your boyish ways, brother—anything in the line of excitement, and you fairly itch to be up and doing. I am free to confess, however, that when you *do* get into a ruction you know how to give a good account of yourself."

"Thanks, ole hoss, comin' from sech as yeou that's the highest kind o' praise I could ever expect. I sometimes reckon I must abeen in at least one squabble 'fore I was hardly able to toddle 'raound, it comes so nat'ral to me."

On the following morning their regular routine was again taken up. They flew up the coast, and turned out to sea, Jack wishing to learn whether there was a mother ship lying off the coast, from which all manner of prohibited articles, from aliens, precious stones, narcotics and in great quantity the finest of foreign strong drink, down to the smallest things that had an intrinsic value, were secretly imported into the States minus the heavy duty imposed on their coming.

Once again his hunch proved a true one, for they discovered a squat steamer hovering about twenty-five miles from the coast, with several fast smuggling power-boats alongside; and as Perk reported, a number of men passing weighty sacks over the side of the larger craft.

"No need of our going any closer, partner," Jack announced, as he banked sharply, and turned the nose of their boat toward the north. "We'll just knock around for a spell, to experience the sensation of slipping along above the great salty sea, something neither of us have had much experience in doing; and in good time we can pass on down again, so as to cover the ground where we expect to get in our heavy work."

Which same they did, to their own satisfaction; and much to Jack's surprise to also discover a second large foreign ship apparently also laden to the gunwales with piles of goods in suspicious looking gunny sacks.

"It seems as though it might be high time something was being done to cut this traffic into ribbons, don't you think, Wally, boy?" Jack asked, as again he made a steep bank, this time heading into the west, toward the distant streak of land which told of the coast of Virginia.

They struck out for shore, passed as far inland as Jack considered tactful, and through his clever work in piloting the airship actually passed directly over Black Water Bayou.

CHAPTER XXI

A Motor-Truck Caravan

"I say, buddy!"

They were bobbing in and out of the fleecy drift clouds, just as that other ship had done, almost undistinguishable from the ground, being about two miles up, when Jack thus called out.

Perk had been taking account as to the amount of fuel yet remaining in their tanks, and was amusing himself doing some sort of calculation with a stub of a pencil and a pad of paper.

"Yeah! what is it, boss?" he sang out, looking over to where his mate sat at the stick, with the exhaust racket of both motors cut-off effectually.

"We're just whiffing over that delightful little ghostly bayou you fell in love with; and heading so as to pass above the region from which we heard that unseen ship settle down."

"I reckoned that was so, partner; go ahead an' say what's on yeour mind."

"There's one thing that so far has escaped our scrutiny," spoke up the pilot, with Perk quickly adding:

"Meanin', I reckons, suh, we aint seen nary a

172

sign o' any sorter vehicle sech as mout be atakin' the stuff to market—is that so, suh?"

"Good guess, all right, for you, Wally, boy," replied Jack. "Pick up your glasses again, and keep an eye on the ground down below. If by good luck you light on anything suspicious, let me know; because I want to see for myself, as it might help me figure out certain things worth while."

"Ay! ay! Cap; here goes!" Perk told him, suiting the action to the words with the greatest eagerness.

Jack loitered somewhat, not wishing to skip over that prospective battlefield too speedily, lest it fail to reveal some of its most valuable secrets; accordingly he circled while still sticking to the cloud screen, now in and out like a fluttering butterfly amidst the thistle blooms of an old quarry.

Their aerial steed could not be seen from the far distant surface of the earth, unless one chanced to have a very powerful pair of binoculars similar to the beautiful ones Perk was just then handling —the Government at least was a generous employer, since the question of price never entered into the purchase of such instruments as were necessary.

Suddenly Perk let out a loud crow.

"Gimme the stick, gov'nor!" he called out, shoving in behind his mate. "Aplenty in sight right naow, I'd say, if yeou asked me. Jest peek yeour eye on that ere stretch o' marsh, I take the same to be, clost alongside yonder stretch o' pine woods —must be some sorter corduroy road built through the muck, screened mostly by cypress trees covered with a heap o' trapsin' moss."

"I've got it, partner—just as you're saying in the bargain, a corduroy road made of logs laid parallel, and looking a bit new as if it had only been constructed lately, for some special purpose."

"See anythin' amovin', boss?" continued the excited Perk, eagerly.

"Not yet," he was told; "but whatever you saw may be hidden behind some patch of dense timber at the moment. Ha!"

"Ketched 'em jest then, did yeou?"

"One—two—three motor-trucks in a line, close to each other, and making fair time over that bumpy log-road, considering that they seem to be heavily laden with something covered by dirty tarpaulins."

"Somethin'—huh! weuns ought to know what kinder stuff, eh, partner?" laughed Perk, jubilantly enough.

"Keep circling around, using these hazy clouds for a screen, whenever possible, brother," urged Jack. "I want to get an eyeful of this same picture, because it's going to give me the one thing that was lacking—a knowledge of the way they get the stuff out of such a boggy country without being detected by sharp-eyed revenue men."

"But say, boss, didn't we make up aour minds they might have a bunch o' landin'-places, so's to switch aroun' when things begun to get too hot at any one roost?"

"Yes, and I still believe that way," Jack told him, his eyes continuing to be glued to his glasses, as though what he saw fairly fascinated him; "but just the same, they could make use of one main road out of the swamp country."

So he kept close tabs until eventually the line of heavily laden trucks had passed from his sight.

"You can pick up the course to Charleston now, buddy," he told the acting pilot. "I've seen that those trucks are heading north by nor-west, and chances are they mean to make Baltimore before they halt for good; though like as not they may have a half-way station for stopping over during part of a day, so as to cover the last and most risky section of their long run by darkness, or moonlight."

"An' partner," Perk blurted out, as he relinquished the stick to the masterhand of his mate, "do yeou know they's somethin' that's been abotherin' me right smart."

"As what, buddy?" asked the other, keeping up his run among the friendly screen of fleecy clouds.

"Things they seem to come an' go with these here smuggler lads like everything might be part o' a well greased machine—never a click, er a squeak, but movin' 'long with hardly a missfire— jest haowever *do* they fix it— how kin they know near to the minute when a cargo's acomin' to port, so's to have them trucks and men awaitin' fo' the same."

"Oh! that's dead easy, partner," Jack sang out, as though on his part he felt little doubt.

"Yeah! seems to me them chaps 'way back in Columbus' time said them same words arter the man as diskivered America stood a egg up on end, fust knockin' the small end, and making a rest fo' the same—anything's soft enough arter you been told haow—naow I wanter be shown."

"Listen then, Wally, boy—there isn't the least doubt in my mind but what the gang has an excellent radio station rigged up somewhere along the coast; they can keep in constant touch both with the mother ships we saw anchored twenty miles out, and also with headquarters on shore— down where those three motor-trucks loaded up, after some speed boat ran in here last night. Get it now, do you, old pal?"

"Gosh! seems like us boys gotter be settin' up nights fixin' traps fo' the sharp foxes, they's up to sech big stunts. Sometimes I find myself wonderin' haow in Sam Hill weuns kin beat 'em atall at their pesky games."

"Well, that's what we're here to put through," Jack stated, off-hand like; "and it seems that usually we do come out on top. But even if we succeed in putting their freight air ships, and fast launches out of business, this game of ours can never be called complete until we've managed to discover the location of that powerful sending radio station— and blown it sky-high in the bargain."

"Bully boy!" cried Perk; "an' more power to aour elbow, is what I'm asayin' right naow, Big Boy. We *kin* do it, an'—watch aour smoke, that's all."

"I begin to think the time for our departure is getting close at hand, Pal Wally," Jack remarked some time later, as they glimpsed the familiar smoke cloud hovering over the city ahead. "If my last talk with our good friend tonight pans out as I feel pretty certain it must, we'll figure on making our big jump some time day after tomorrow. That will give us plenty of time to get everything aboard we expect to need; for once we leave Charleston we'll not be likely to see the place again in a hurry."

"Sure pleases me a heap, suh," Perk told him, nodding his head approvingly, as though he might be some species of war-horse scenting the battle-smoke and acrid odor of burnt powder in the breeze, calling him to action.

In due time the big amphibian dropped down on the field, and was hurriedly conveyed to its hangar; the two airmen hovering around for a brief time examining certain parts of their ship, to make doubly certain there was nothing amiss. Jack did not intend going out on the following day, if things worked as he was now planning; they would fix up a last day program, by following which everything necessary would be carried out in the customary way of such careful adventurers as they had always proven to be.

"Huh! been a right full day, I'd call hit," was Perk's last word, as they started back to the hotel, so as to clean up for supper; after which Jack meant to keep an engagement with Mr. Herriott, who would be apt to have some news of importance to communicate.

"Taking things as they go, it certainly has, brother," Jack told his "side push," as Perk often called himself. "We've picked up some facts that plug the vacant holes in my scheme; and I feel confident we're getting close to the big finish."

CHAPTER XXII

Down to Business at Last

When Jack came back to the hotel late that night, he found Perk lounging in the lobby, and keeping a watchful eye on the main entrance.

"Got too darned lonesome up in the den, suh," the latter explained, keeping up his character part as an employee of the rich New York sportsman, who was so well liked that he had become a sort of companion, and campmate in fact. "Jest couldn't stand it any longer, an' had to come daown hyah, so's to watch the folks, an' pass the time away. Gwine up right naow, suh?"

"Might just as well, for I'm a bit tired; and besides we have some plans to settle on before striking out for the ducking grounds day after tomorrow. Got those chilled-shot shells I want to try out, did you, Wally?"

"Sure did, suh," answered the other, with a wide grin, knowing that this had been spoken because the hotel clerk was close by at the desk, and watching them a bit curiously. "An' I done reckoned as haow I might jest as well fotch 'long double the number o' boxes yeou-all asked me to. They sure slips away right speedy like, suh, when the birds air atradin' good."

Once behind the closed and locked door, Jack started to explain such fresh facts as had come within the circle of his knowledge in the last chat with Mr. Herriott.

"He will make all arrangements with Jethro in the morning, so we can expect to find the man waiting at the rendezvous—Black Water Bayou, two nights from now; for I calculate to drop down there just while the twilight holds. That is the main thing we settled; and he assured me there would absolutely be no hitch to that part of the program. When such a man as our good friend gives a promise like that you can depend on it being exactly so."

"Bet yeour boots that's a fack, partner," Perk took occasion to add most fervently, having conceived a great liking for Mr. Herriott, his charming betterhalf, and the two youngsters with whom he had had such a riotous time on the occasion of his late visit.

Jack took some object out of his pocket, and holding it between his fingers seemed to blow softly into the same with a certain quavering inflection. The result was an odd quacking sound, several times repeated.

"Gosh all hemlock!" Perk exclaimed, a little too

loud for discretion as he himself appeared to realize, since he immediately moderated his voice as he went on to say: "If that ere aint a reg'lar duck-call I'm a rank piker. What dye know 'baout that, if we didn't forgit to supply aourselves with a quacker—two on 'em in fact, one to coax the ducks within gunshot; an' tother fo' wild honkin' geese. Takes yeou to think up the small but important things, ole hoss."

"Well, we may some day have a chance to use this call for the purpose it was intended," stated Jack, handing the queer little article with the split and brass tongue crown over to Hank for examination; "but I got it for quite another reason. When I put this to my lips, and give a number of loud quacks, it'll be after we're lying there on the surface of Black Water Bayou—as a signal agreed on with Jethro. You must remember he has never met us, unfortunately, and this game is too risky for any one to take chances. He'll answer my signal by six quacks in quick succession, and I'll give him another four in reply—then both will have made sure covering the identity of the other."

"Jest fine as silk, I'd say, suh!" Perk assured him, with that look approaching adoration such as came to him most naturally, whenever his pal Jack sprang some unusually neat piece of work upon him.

Perk tested the duck-call several times, blowing softly, so as not to cause any guest, or possibly even a spy, in an adjoining room to wonder what such a series of queer sounds could mean.

"Huh! been a long time, suh, since I done used one o' these contraptions," he finally advanced. "They do fotch the s'picious birds aswimmin' closer in to the stools—yeou knows I gotter to buy a bunch o' cedar decoys tomorry, 'case no shooter ever goes aout to bag ducks withaout a flock o' the same."

"That's down on your list of last supplies to be picked up, I remember, Wally. And when I've told you a few more things that come to me tonight we'd better turn in for a good snatch of sleep. No telling how much time we'll be spending keeping wide-awake night after night, once we embark on that part of our big game. In fact, it's possible we'll have to change things around, and do about all of our sleeping daytimes."

"Suits me right well, suh—so long's I gits fo' hours at a stretch, with a few halfway decent eats thrown in, I doant never kick."

Less than half an hour later and they were getting ready for a spell of forgetfulness. Perk, as he crawled into bed, was muttering something to the effect that there would be only one more occasion when they could treat themselves to the real luxury of a decent bed, with a fine bathroom conveniently close at hand.

"But what do it matter with sech a ole campaigner as *me*—anything we kin strike aint agoin' to be one-tenth as bad as when I was over in them stinkin' trenches, up to my knees in water, an' listenin' to hell broke loose all raound, with the Heinies throwing shiploads o' shells, an' other devilish explosives—awful pizen gas in the bargain, every-which way—I ain't complainin' o' anything after what happened to me there, no siree, I aint."

In the morning they took a leisurely breakfast, and then separated, each of them having a complete list of certain necessary things that had to be attended to.

Jack had declared it his intention to take-off around midday, for they could once more follow the course now becoming quite familiar—passing out to sea, and from a great hight learning whether a mother-ship lay off the coast, with fast speedboats tied up alongside, taking on cargoes—although no attempt would be made looking to coming in to the mouth of some estuary, up which they meant to push under cover of darkness.

Only one thing could keep them from making their start as planned, and this would be a bad weather report covering the coastal region from

Brunswick, Georgia all the way past Hatteras, to the mouth of the Delaware. Optimistic Jack, however, was hoping for the best, since as far as he could see no bad weather appeared on the latest report from Headquarters, as given in the Charleston papers.

Much was accomplished during the morning, and both of them brought back various packages that were to be carried in their bags to the field, at the time of taking off.

"You looked after those decoys, I expect, brother?" Jack queried, as they sat at the lunch table, enjoying all manner of good things appealing to their sound appetites.

"Better b'lieve I did that same, buddy," the other assured him; "an' a mighty likely lookin' bunch o' stools I picked up. They're sendin' the same to the aviation grounds this afternoon; an' I'm meanin' to run aout so's to stow the wooden ducks away aboard aour ship. I'd give somethin' for a chanct to shoot over them same decoys, yes suh, I sure would."

"Perhaps fortune will be kind to us, and you may yet have that pleasure, Pal Wally. No telling but what we may be ordered to hang out around this part of the coast for some time after we've done our job to the Queen's taste; and to tell you the truth I'd enjoy a little shooting myself.

The afternoon passed, and when the sun sank low in the west, with their coming together again at the hotel, never a single item on either list had been neglected.

In the morning Jack walked around to the post-office where the latest weather reports could be found, to see if they corresponded with the rosy promises the morning papers contained. He assured Perk on returning that they need have no fears about making the start as scheduled; so that Perk found his cup of happiness full to the brim, and even running over.

They took an early lunch and then went out to the aviation grounds in a taxi as usual. Before their ship was trundled out to be set for a start they saw that everything was aboard, and safely stowed away, from the cumbersome decoy flock to the last thing in "chow," as selected by capable Perk, about as good a judge with regard to food supplies as could be run across in a day's search.

The manager of the aviation field himself was out to shake hands, and give them a parting good-bye. Jack, seeing the smile accompanying the words and hearty handclasp, had a faint suspicion that possibly the affable gentleman had guessed something like the truth; but just the same he felt it would never go any further, if he could read good Southern faith in a human's eyes.

CHAPTER XXIII

At the Rendezvous

The big amphibian, well loaded down, made a creditable take-off, and they were soon mounting up toward cloudland. As on the previous occasion there chanced to be a never ending flock of beautiful white fleecy clouds passing along, with the sun shining most of the time, since the banks of vapor were "light-weight," as Perk poetically described them.

Looking back Perk took his last view of Charleston, a bit regretfully, since the quaint aspects of the city, connected with oldtime buildings, and other agreeable sights, had somehow gripped his heart.

Jack again soon headed off the coast, it being his intention, if the conditions were at all favorable, to drop down on the sea, and float there, waiting until the afternoon was well advanced before heading in to the shore.

After they had passed for many miles up the coast he picked out a spot—after being warned by the lookout that there were two large vessels standing off beyond the twenty-mile line, undoubtedly mother-ships loaded down with fresh supplies of contraband—where they could lie upon the surface of the water undetected by any one passing far above, or at such a distance away as the foreign ships appeared to lie.

Jack could not remember having ever known the restless Atlantic to remain almost perfectly calm for such a long stretch of time—he felt like taking it as a favorable sign concerning the carrying out of their individual great plan—even the elements were apparently in league to render them assistance, which he took it to be most kind and reassuring on their part.

Along about three in the afternoon Perk, again searching everywhere for some sort of discovery, announced that he had picked out a plane ducking in and out of the white battalions of clouds still passing overhead.

"Seems like she might be acomin' from that quarter where we got aour hunch the landin' field o' their airships must lie," he went on to say, as though his mind was made up along those lines. "Reckon as haow they caint pick weuns off daown hyah, suh, seein' aour wings air abaout the same color as the sea all 'raound this same spot."

"Not the least chance of such a thing, partner," Jack assured him; "I had them colored that way purposely, seeing that we'd be likely to squat down this way when spying on the mother ship further out—not even if they have binoculars aboard, which they undoubtedly must, could any one make us out. Heading for that foreign steamship, isn't that cloud chaser?"

"Straight away, suh, as sure as shootin'. Course they reckon on loadin' up with somethin' that's aboard, an' wants to git ashore the wust kind—mebbe a bunch o' Chinks it might be; or else some sorter stuff like high-toned laces, Cape diamonds, or sech expensive big things as allers come in small packages."

"At any rate," Jack went on to mention, "they are heading for one of those two foreign boats further out. You say there were several speed boats and launches fast to the sides of the big freighters, when you glimpsed them? Strikes me things are breaking about right for our making a start in the big racket tonight—of course depending on Jethro's bobbing up all serene."

Perk followed the course of the airship dipping in and out of the cloud belt, and after quite some time had elapsed made his announcement.

"They sure is acomin' daown ashootin', Big Boss. Reckons as haow there must be a good hand at that ere stick, a lad as knows his business okay—there, he's flattened aout, an' takes things some easier, seein' as haow the ship's ready to make contact with the sea. Aint this a reg'lar picnic o'

a time, when weuns kin jest lay here like a gull
afloatin' on the water, an' see haow them smugglin'
devils work things. Little do they suspect that
there's sumpin' hangin' heavy over ther heads, an'
liable to crash any ole minit from naow on."

It was by now getting close to the time Jack
figured on making a start. He planned on taking a
leaf from the routine methods brought into service
by the expert pilots manning the illegal air carriers, passing in and out from mother ship to their
secret landing place—by making a high ceiling,
and depend on a curtain of lofty clouds to effectually screen their presence while hopping over the
danger zone.

"Time we skipped out of this," he told Perk,
who emitted a muffled roar which was possibly
meant to be an expression akin to applause.

The waves were picking up somewhat in the
bargain, which may have been one of the reasons
why the ever cautious Jack wanted to get moving:
he did not have any particular yearning for a head-
long dash amidst rolling billows, such as might
cause considerable trouble, even bring risk in their
train should they find themselves compelled to
make the venture.

However, they made the ascent without great
trouble, even if there was a certain amount of
splashing done. Perk looked pleased when the ship

arose from its salt water contact, and began climbing at a steady pace.

Jack held out for some little time as though meaning to pass inshore far to the north of the point he was really aiming to attain; this he did to hoodwink any one who might chance to see them through strong glasses, and feel a little curious to know who they were, also, what their object could be in carrying on after such a fashion.

Eventually he turned more into the west; then, after passing over the shore line, faced due southwest, and sped on.

Finally when Perk warned them they were approaching their proposed landing-place Jack brought his charge lower until presently, as evening drew on apace, they could be seen sweeping along not five hundred feet above the tops of the tall cypress trees with their queer festoons of trailing Spanish moss.

Then came a glimpse of Black Water Bayou, bordered by the mysterious gloomy looking swamp, from whence had come all those uncouth sounds on the occasion of their stopover some time previously.

"Huh! mebbe we'll git right 'customed to them awful noises," Perk was assuring himself, as their pontoons glided along the smooth surface of the lonely lagoon, and the boat headed directly toward that artificial curtain behind which they had previously pocketed their "windjammer," or as Perk sometimes called their craft the "crocodile"— partly because, as he affirmed, such a reptile was the only real amphibian, able to negotiate both land and water in turn, and feeling at home in both.

"So far, okay," he observed, softly, after the boat had come to a stop, close to that friendly ambush where they could readily hide their craft should they choose to start forth with Jethro aboard his smaller ducking powerboat; "an' naow let's on'y hope the gink shows up on time."

"I wouldn't speak of Jethro in that sort of way, buddy," remonstrated Jack. "It's true he is a Southern cracker, without much education; but that I'd call his misfortune and not his fault. Mr. Herriott says he's a chap with considerable principle, and his one weakness is about the wrongs this bunch of men have done him and his family. He is ready to encounter every risk if only he can show them up, cripple their big business, and possibly send some of the lot to Atlanta for a term of years."

"I get yeou, partner," said Perk, contritely; "shore didn't mean anything by sayin' what I did; an' I'll be glad to shake Jethro's flipper whensoever we meet."

"I knew you'd feel that way, Wally; and it may

not be a great many minutes before the chance comes along."

"Meanin', I take it, Boss, he orter show up right soon?" demanded the other.

"This is the rendezvous place you know, where we agreed to wait for him," explained Jack; "he may be a bit late getting up here, for his boat is an old one; though Mr. Herriott did tell me he himself had had it fixed up some, to work a lot smoother—Uncle Sam stood the racket, too; and you know when *he* foots a bill nothing is too good to be utilized. We may be surprised when we see that same dinky powerboat."

"As haow, partner?" queried Perk, his curiosity aroused immediately.

"Wait and see, brother," Jack told him, tantalizingly. "Our first duty right now is to poke the nose of our airship back of this dandy natural curtain, where it just couldn't be seen, unless a close search was being made, our plans possibly having been given away. That couldn't happen in a coon's age, we've been so cautious, so secretive, and made no confidents except Mr. Herriott— and through him necessarily Jethro. Take hold, and help me swing her along back of the trailing moss and vines."

When this had been effected Jack again whispered:

"Listen while I give the signal, partner; if by any chance hostile ears were to catch the quacking of a duck, it could hardly excite the slightest notice; for such a sound often breaks out in the darkness of night down here, since a duck on the water acts as sentry to the sleeping flock. Here goes, then:"

CHAPTER XXIV

PERK RIDES IN THE GHOST BOAT

"Quack—quack—quack—quack!"

Perk chuckled at the clever way Jack imitated the outcry of a startled feathered pilgrim from the Far North—old shooter as he was, Perk felt confident he himself would have been deceived did he not know whence the sounds proceeded.

He listened intently, hoping they might not be disappointed in their expectations. There came an answering call from a point close by—it gave Perk a positive thrill—then Jethro must have already arrived, spurred on by his burning desire to pay his debt of hatred long since over due.

Jack waited a dozen seconds, after which he again sent out his call, repeating the first one exactly—four quacks.

"Gee whiz! somepin's amovin' over yonder, matey!" whispered the excited Perk, as they peered through openings in the leafy curtain by which the airship was so deftly concealed.

"I see it," answered Jack, also feeling a thrill of satisfaction, in that their great scheme gave positive indications of being about to start off with a bang. "It's some sort of boat okay—too dark yet to tell just what shape the same may be. There, it's coming out of hiding now."

"An' a powerboat in the bargain—Jethro's crate, I shore reckons; but hot-diggetty-dig! see haow fast she's a headin' thisaway, yet yeou caint ketch even a ripple, or hear the exhaust one teeny bit. A ghost boat, I'd call her, partner, blamed if I wouldn't."

Jack chuckled as if amused.

"Mr. Herriott put me wise about that," he explained, softly. "It's one of the big improvements Uncle Sam brought about in that old craft, in order that it could do the work so much better—and safer. You see, the overboard motor that's been installed in place of the old one is up-to-date, and has its exhaust away down deep, so it can swing along without any of the racket most powerboats kick up. It's used a great deal by fishermen, who troll for game-fish, and would expect but scant captures if their boat kept spluttering away as the old type used to do. Get that now, Wally?"

"Jest what I do, ole pal; an' say, aint it won-der-ful what things they're inventin' these days—talk 'bout there bein' nawthin' new under the sun, why, hardly a day slips past that we doant hear or read 'baout stunnin' discoveries. That certain is a happy thought. But here he is, clost to us, pard."

"Hello! thar!" came in a low, discreet voice, as the oncoming boat slowed up by degrees.

"It's okay, Jethro—we're on hand as promised!"

As Jack said this the other gave a low laugh, as though greatly pleased to find his new employer so prompt, and evidently a man of his word.

He was soon leaning from his seat in the cockpit of his ancient powerboat, (in which he had for some years been engaged taking parties out from Charleston for their fishing, or shooting) and grasping first the extended hand of eager Perk, then that of Jack Ralston.

He had been put wise as to their real identity, but warned to meet them under their assumed names, so as to ward off any possible risk of discovery. So it was he lowered his voice to a hoarse whisper as he spoke after the handshake.

"Ah 'low as how yuh reckoned ah mout be some slow agittin' hyah, suh; but since they fixed up my ole dickey boat, she shore do step along like smoke."

"Glad to know that, Jethro," said Jack, to whom the other had turned as if readily recognizing which of the pair must be the leader of the desperate enterprize with which he had committed his fortunes so gladly. "Looks like a fine night for us to make a beginning."

"Jest what hit is, suh; couldn't be no better, ah'd say. An' ah done reckons as how they be some big doin's goin' on over tuh the station ter-night."

"That sounds good to me, Jethro," Jack assured him. "Fact is, I'm beginning to believe the Fates are working in our favor right along, from the way things keep happening. Now I'm going to put the work in your hands as far as getting us in touch with these parties goes."

"I kinder figgered as how yuh'd do thet same, suh," said the confident Jethro, "seein' as how I knows the ground like er book. I aint agoin' tuh let yuh down, suh, bet yuh boots I aint."

Perk had not tried to break into this brief con-fab; truth to tell he was engaged just then in keep-ing "tabs" on Jethro's manner of speech, so as to determine how close to the real thing he himself had come when trying to play the part of a genuine Birmingham son of Dixie.

"How are we going to start this racket?" ques-tioned Jack. "All get in your boat, and close in on the working station, so we can see with our own eyes just what sort of a show they're putting up."

"Them's ther ticket, suh," he was promptly told, showing that the guide had formed some sort of a general plan of campaign. "I be'n right up agin the level groun' whar them airships land, an' watched what was happenin' lots o' times. 'Taint no great shakes agittin' clost tuh thet workin' bunch, 'case they don't reckon they's a single stranger inside o' ten mile. They'd shore skun me alive if they'd run ontuh me; but I knowed my beans, an' how tuh fool ther best o' 'em."

Jack liked the way the other talked—it showed that Jethro had considerable self-confidence; also that the consuming passion running like hot lava through his veins was not apt to warp his judgment in the least. He could be depended on to keep fairly cool and discreet under any trying condition; and should matters ever come to a showdown, such a man would fight like a South Carolina wildcat, of that Jack also felt assured.

"Then we'll leave the ship concealed here back of this screen, and climb aboard with you, Jethro," Jack told him. "I put it up to you to say when we ought to make a start."

"Right away'd be ther right thing ter do, suh," came the answer; after both Jack and Perk had changed to the reconditioned powerboat. "Yuh see, it's sum way tuh go, the river's so crooked in places; so I kalc'late things they'll be fair hummin' by ther time we gits thar."

"Just as you say, Jethro; but perhaps we ought to take certain things with us—no telling just how soon we might find a use for the same. Wally, climb back, and pass them over to me—you know what I mentioned I'd like to have along."

Evidently Perk had committed the list to memory, for he handed the articles over in rapid succession—guns, along with other things that must have been a rank mystery to the staring Jethro, though he made no remark.

"That's all, Big Boss," observed Perk, once more changing to the powerboat, and the seat he had just started to warm up.

Not the ghost of a sound of passing vapor came to Perk's strained ears as the boat picked up a certain amout of speed, heading directly for the near-by river, which Jack had called the Yamasaw. Perk could hardly believe there could be such a thing as throttling the noisy clamor he had always associated with the passage of a motorboat, usually heard over the water from a distance of several miles. Truly the wizards must be hard at work these days, performing near-miracles right and left—first the aircraft's noisy discharge conquered; and now the humble powerboat reduced to absolute submission.

Jack quickly noticed that Jethro was making no great attempt to force his smoothly working new engine. He could conceive of several good reasons for this caution—in the first place there was no need for haste; then again they would be going with the rapid current while descending the crooked stream; and last of all he could readily

understand how there might be a variety of obstacles here and there, blocking their passage—
logs, and huge boulders, which would surely cause
the boat to founder, should they crash against some
snag head-on.

On the return journey, whenever they chose to
come back, the case must be different, since they
would have the current to buck against, and necessarily much more power would be called upon to
make decent progress.

However, Jack was not figuring as to just when
that retrograde movement would come about—
Perk had handed over a variety of things they
would require if they chose to linger for a day
and another night at least, even to some "eats"—
catch Perk neglecting *that* part of the supplies—
not if he was in his sane mind, he had told himself
with unction.

Well, here they were gliding along down the
river, just as Perk had so many times vividly pic-
tured in his mind, with darkness all around them,
and only Jethro's intimate knowledge of the in-
tricacies of the stream, and its various outjutting
snags, standing between themselves and a cold
bath.

Perk thrilled with deepest satisfaction. From
this time on he felt assured all sorts of exciting
happenings would be the order of the day or night;

and no longer would he feel bored by inaction. The war against the desperate smuggler gang was on, and the outcome could not possibly be delayed much longer than forty-eight hours, he felt confident.

Half an hour and more had now passed since their start on the inland voyage, and several times they found the angry water foaming up around them as if eager to drag the adventurous voyagers down into its unknown depths. But always Jethro maintained a perfect grasp on the situation, parrying this rock, and that snag, as though he possessed the eyes of a cat.

It was simply amazing how he managed, and Perk found himself growing deeper and deeper wrapped up in sincere admiration for one who could display such wonderful skill, such fearless handling of a frail boat in all that turgid, leaping water.

Finally Jethro began to slow up, and the others knew from this that evidently they must be drawing close to the place for which they were aiming. Yes, several times when it happened the water was more calm, Perk felt positive he caught the faint sound of human voices, as though reckless men might be making merry with some sort of liquid refreshment that loosened their tongues, and made them feel unusually jolly.

So, too, did he glimpse signs of growing light, and figured that doubtless fires might be burning, with supper cooking. Fed up with a desire to set eyes on what lay so close by, Perk counted the minutes as the boat continued to move smoothly along.

Finally he found that Jethro was propelling it by hand, the noiseless engine having stopped its pulsations; and a minute later they lay back of a screen formed of hanging Spanish moss and clinging vines, quite as effectual so far as concealment went as the curtain hiding the airship.

"Git out hyah, suh;" whispered Jethro in Jack's ear; "rest o' ther way we gotter tuh go afoot."

CHAPTER XXV

A WELL OILED MACHINE

One thing in particular Jack had noticed—this was the fact that shortly before this stop had been made they had left the main stream, and pushed up some smaller subsidiary, although the water seemed to be quite deep.

He had found it easy to understand just how speedboats, loaded down to the gunnels with sacks of contraband, were able to come up from the mouth of the Yamasaw, and make their passage safe by means of searchlights on board for that particular purpose—since they must invariably choose the night for making their depot, and eluding such searching Coast Patrol revenue cutters as were on duty in those shore waters.

It made Jack smile to think how in turn he was heading a swift patrol of the air, inaugurated to sweep this audacious combine from the sea, and break up the powerful syndicate so long defying the Government.

"It's now got down to brass tacks," he was telling himself, as with Perk at his side he carefully followed at the heels of the crawling cracker guide; "and a case of dog eat dog, as Perk would call it; so I only hope our canine will act the part of a German police, or shepherd dog, and eat up the other beast, that's all."

The closer they drew to the camp of the smugglers the more Jethro drew upon his education as a skillful tracker and guide to avoid discovery. Perk, taking occasional sly peeps, could make out a number of rough-looking men moving here and there, as though restless; and from this fact he felt confident they must be waiting for the arrival of something that had to do with their presence here in this isolated camp.

Yes, and presently he also discovered several huge motor trucks parked nearby, the presence of which settled the matter; for he knew positively a laden speedboat must be on the way, probably bucking against the current of the river at that identical minute. If they stood by their guns the best part of the night they might witness a transfer of the contraband from boat to truck; and, if very lucky, even pick up some information regarding the destination of the double load.

When finally Jethro came to a halt they were really as close to the camp as the lay of the ground on that side would permit, without taking too risky chances for discovery.

Perk was soon pulling at Jack's sleeve as if de-

sirous of attracting his comrade's attention. Seeing that the other was so persistent Jack inclined
his ear as a sign for the other to only speak in the
faintest possible whisper, which of course Perk
only too well knew was absolutely necessary.

"Looky—over there jest back o' thet tree, an'
away from the fires—aint that some sorter crate
yeou kin lamp?"

"Just what it is, a plane, and a whopping big one
to boot," Jack assured him, when he could find
Perk's ear. "No seaplane after all, so it can't be
used for going out to the mother ship; but flies
over the land, taking some sort of stuff to a certain
depot—may have fetched a bunch of Chinks over
from Cuba on its last trip. Keep still, now, Wally,
and just watch."

The time dragged on until several hours had
passed since they arrived at the landing field and
camp of those busy bees engaged in hoodwinking
Uncle Sam, and all his efficient coast patrol both on
sea and the land.

Then a throbbing sound reached their ears; at
the same time they could notice how the men no
longer rough-housed among themselves. On the
contrary they began to gather at a small wharf
built so that a boat could draw alongside, and let
the cargo be transferred to the waiting trucks for
further transportation.

Perk again touched his best pal's arm, to whisper:

"Boat's a kickin' up agin the current, an' gettin' nigh here," he said.

"Okay, but put a stopper on your tongue, matey —eyes are all we need right now—maybe ears as well, to pick up anything that's said worth while."

Thus crushed Perk fell back, and concentrated his observation upon the stirring little night drama that would soon be moving along at full speed— a common enough event it must be, judging by the long security from interruption these reckless worthies had enjoyed.

The strong glare of a large searchlight down on the waterway grew brighter continually, showing that the approaching boat must be close at hand. Presently they were able to make her out, although almost dazzled by the brilliant light up in her bow, rendered necessary by the snags and rocks scattered at intervals all along the Yamasaw.

No sooner had the boat been warped to the dock than men flocked aboard, and began to tote the heaped-up heavy sacks ashore. There could be not the shadow of a doubt concerning the nature of their contents, for occasionally the eagerly listening trio caught the sound of flint glass striking against a similar clinking object; and when one sack seemed to accidentally come open, Jack caught the sheen of the light on a serried row of bottles, all bearing foreign labels. He even saw the man carrying the same swiftly crib a bottle, and conceal it under a friendly strip of wood, as though laying by a means for conviviality at a later hour.

Taken in all it was a rather tempting spectacle for a pair of Secret Service bloodhounds to find spread out before their admiring eyes. Jack was priming his ears so as to catch any careless words spoken by these men landing the cargo fetched from one of those mother ships standing by off the shore. Even a name spoken would be treasured in hopes of it eventually turning the scrutiny of Uncle Sam's vigilant enforcers of the revenue laws upon some party, who thus far had never once been suspected as allied with this formidable conspiracy.

It did not take very long for the numerous workers to clear the decks and hold of the numerous staunch burlap sacks, each of which must have held possibly a full dozen quart bottles.

Some four stout men, apparently the crews of the two big motortrucks, kept busy loading the stuff aboard their cars. Evidently they meant to cover the entire load under some hay that was heaped up close by, possibly fetched for this very purpose, the whole being well tucked down under a dingy looking but stout tarpaulin that could be roped securely by expert hands.

Yes, it was certainly all very interesting, and instructive as well, but then the three watchers were no novices, all of them having witnessed similar sights many times in the past.

At least Jack had reason to believe certain things that floated to his ears,—mostly names being mentioned by some of the talkative workers—might prove strong clues, that, being followed up to their logical conclusion, would bring interesting developments later on.

This encouraged him very much, as he realized he was now in a position to reap some sort of harvest to pay for the hard work he had been putting in.

Now that the speed boat had been cleared of its heavy load there were movements aboard looking to a departure. It being already past midnight perhaps the master of the blockade runner—having been duly posted through some obscure means— knew just about where the Government vessel from which he had the most to fear would be cruising at that hour; and figured it would be a wise move on his part to gain the high seas as soon as convenient.

Perk saw these actions with falling spirits— he had been so sure Jack meant to begin operations without any delay that to thus let that swift contraband runner get away unscathed was really too bad.

So he had to crouch there behind the network of bushes, and see the vessel back away from the rough-looking dock, swing around in the narrow but deep creek, and then disappear down-stream, the light of its glowing reflector gradually dying out as it drew farther away.

"Huh! nawthin' doin' seems like," Perk was telling himself in bitter disappointment. "I'd a given a heap jest to slip one o' my bally time-bombs aboard that ere craft, so she'd bust into flames when far away down the river; but Jack, he doant seem ready to hit the fust crack."

Next the two laden trucks pulled out, and could be heard bumping along the road, to take their chances of getting through without being stopped by either high-jackers or revenue men.

"Makin' straight fo' that same corduroy road as runs plumb through the marsh; an' headin' due north, too," Perk further told himself, seeing that evidently trying to talk with his chum was taboo for the time being, "Goin' up to Baltimore, I reckon, whar they got a big taste fo' strong stuff, 'specially sech as comes in from abroad—reg'lar goods, with a big kick backin' same. Huh!"

Jack had for some little time been looking earnestly first at the nearest campfire, and then diverting his gaze, seemed to stare over to where the outlaw plane rested. It was as though it might be waiting for some particular event, when possibly it would start off, after taking aboard certain valuables that would come by another airship from some point in the West Indies, evading the customs, and giving a rich bonanza to whoever was interested in thus beating the Government revenue.

"I say, Perk," he whispered in the ear of his mate.

The other must have sensed something of unusual importance coming, for he displayed considerable eagerness as he moderated his own voice to its very lowest pitch, and made answer:

"On deck, suh!"

"That plane—I've been noticing how it's left high and dry there," Jack was saying, significantly, Perk thought.

"Shore is, suh," the latter went on, invitingly.

"I figure that any clever lad might be able to creep close to the same—coming along by that line of bushes you can notice on the side away from the fires, and the big searchlights they use when a ship is taking off at night."

"Easy—reg'lar snap, I'd say, suh."

"I've also figured out that it wouldn't be impossible for any clever lad to creep around from here without being seen, and so get in close grips with that same plane—how?"

Perk lifted his head a trifle, and appeared to study the conditions, which was not at all surprising since up to that minute it had never once occurred to him there would be any call upon him for such services.

"I'd be tickled pink to tackle the job, suh—jest try me!" he finally declared, and at that without even asking why such a dangerous mission should enter into the head of his superior.

"Can you first of all sneak back to the boat, and pick up that little bottle you filled with gasoline before we left the Crocodile?"

"Easy as all get aout, that's right, suh."

"Well, make sure you've got plenty of matches that strike without making any snap," warned Jack; "because we have a chance to get rid of the first outlaw airship, and so make our initial dent in the ironclad syndicate!"

CHAPTER XXVI
STRIKING OUT

Jack was able to say all he did simply because they were separated from the nearest group of men by considerable distance; moreover, the pack persisted in talking and laughing, as though absolutely free from care, doubtless filled with the belief that their lot was a most enviable one— which apparently was the case.

Perk kept as tight a rein on his enthusiasm as he possibly could. He understood just what a perilous mission Jack was entrusting to his sole care; and how success, or failure, would depend on his ability to measure up to the confidence reposed in him.

"Jest where am I to meet up with yeou agin, after I finish my job, suh?" he whispered; even trying to carry out his assumed character when there was really no need for such a thing, showing how the habit was apparently getting a pretty stiff grip on Perk, it would seem.

"When I think it's about time for you to start things going, we'll slip away, so as to be on our road when the fun gets hot and furious; they might begin to scour the whole neighborhood if they suspected some enemy of starting the racket. So look for us where Jethro's boat's hidden. Hold on, partner—come to think of it, give us a bit of a signal when you're on the job—nothing to attract their attention, you understand—just hold up your red handkerchief; but don't wave it, remember. Then three minutes after you've done this—get busy!"

"Huh! leave that to me, boss—I gotter hunch a'ready jest haow that I kin work the game. So-long!"

So matter-of-fact way his leave taking, so informal, that it was plain to be seen Perk must be taking things coolly; a fact that pleased his chum vastly, Jack told himself as the other crept away, heading along the back trail, and making no more noise than a writhing cotton-mouth moccasin snake might have done.

Jack and Jethro waited as the minutes crept past. The latter being advised in low whispers just what was on the bill of fare, might have been heard to chuckle to himself when he finally understood—possibly he was feeling a bit disappointed because this particular mission had not been turned over to his care; but then he must have realized that he was having a share in everything that was attempted looking to the smashing of the powerful smuggler league, which conviction would give him the degree of satisfaction he craved.

Jack could not see how the minutes passed—the lack of good light prevented him from calculating from what the dial of his little wrist watch marked; so, having nothing else to do he commenced counting the seconds, and mentally figuring just how far Perk might have progressed.

Now he would probably be creeping along into the density of the heavier growth, following the sinuosities of the path Jethro had led them along —later on Jack decided the other half of the Crocodile's crew would have arrived at the spot where Jethro's powerboat was hidden back of the friendly natural screen.

He gave Perk a certain stretch of time to gather what he had come after; and then in his mind followed him all the way back to the vicinity of the hostile camp.

For amusement Jack had many a time trained his fancy along such paths as he was now following out; so that really he had become quite an expert in painting similar mind pictures.

And now Perk must be diligently following up his maneuvers by sneaking along on hands and knees, keeping well out of the sight of those carousing near the blazing fires.

When in the nature of things Jack finally concluded the other should have reached his objective, he craned his neck, and started to keep close tabs on the motionless airplane.

Even as he thus looked he discovered a small object that he felt sure could be nothing else than Perk's dingy old bandanna, which he so often wore about his neck, cowboy fashion, when on duty aboard their crate.

One minute he saw this object, and then it vanished utterly from view. Well, that fact rendered his belief more certain—Perk was on deck as big as life; and in three minutes more he would have struck home—it was time he and Jethro were fading out of the picture—making a silent exit from the scene, and be on their way.

So Jack touched his companion on the arm, and began to creep off, with the other close after him.

They succeeded in passing from the near vicinity of the illumination inside the appointed three minutes, after which Jack listened intently as he kept moving, ready to be duly thrilled by an outbreak and commotion announcing the discovery of the blazing crate there on the sloping runway.

Just as he figured it all turned out—without warning loud yells and whoops rang out, telling that every man-jack in the camp must have suddenly made the tremendous discovery that their waiting plane was wrapped in fiercely devouring flames; for the gasoline which Perk had so carefully scattered here and there, would make a wonderful blaze on contact with fire.

Jack found himself speculating how Perk must have managed so as to be on his way, possibly already secure back of the dense thicket, before the fire broke out; but all that could be explained later on.

He remembered what the other had said about having a "hunch"; and Jack, knowing how fertile his pal was in originating bright schemes, felt certain he had been able to rise to the occasion.

He found himself laughing softly as the dreadful clamor rose higher and higher. In imagination he could even see how the startled smuggler crowd must be forced to keep their distance from the costly airship that was being reduced to ashes right before their eyes, with nothing to be done about it, such was the scorching heat accompanying the holocaust.

When it was all over, with nothing remaining save the useless engine of the burned plane, doubtless there would follow a perfect hurricane of surmises as to how so mysterious a fire could have started. The most reasonable conclusion naturally would be that some spark from their camp fires might have been wafted toward the airship, and, still retaining its vigor, fallen upon a tiny pool of inflammable gasoline spilled when the tank had been last replenished.

Let them think what they pleased, it mattered nothing to Jack—the one prime object of his self congratulation lay in the fact that their initial blow had been struck, and the contraband carriers of the air reduced by one useful factor.

The volume of the shouts was gradually becoming less and less; which fact must have resulted from their placing more distance between themselves and the aroused camp; also through the men ceasing to give voice to their excitement, under the conviction that there was no possible remedy for the disaster—and then again the Combine, being swollen with gross profits, could stand such a loss, so easily replaced.

In due time Jack and Jethro approached their goal. It was to be hoped they would find Perk already there; or that he must show up soon after they arrived. They lay among the bushes, and waited, Jack knowing Perk would be apt to give a certain little sound, very like the cheep of a night bird, such as they had frequently used under similar conditions.

A few minutes later sure enough he caught the expected signal, which, upon being immediately answered brought a stooping figure reeling into view. Jack hastened to reach for his chum's right hand which he wrung with considerable unction.

"Good old Perk—you filled the bill okay, I'm telling you, my pal! That's one ship less for them to use in their business—we've made a small dent in their armor, and let's hope there's plenty more still coming to them."

Perk, though breathing hard, was also emitting queer sounds that announced his feeling of complete satisfaction. Jethro also insisted on giving him a generous handshake, to let him know how tickled he felt over seeing those he hated so fiercely meet with their first loss.

"Gosh all hemlock! but things did work smooth, let me tell you-all," Perk finally gasped, unable to repress his exultant feelings any longer, despite his lack of wind. "Say, she whooped things up right stunnin', when the slow match it got its work in—I'd say she did fellers!"

"Slow-match, did you say, brother?" asked Jack, having been given a hint on catching that significant word.

"Shore thing, ole hoss," Perk told him, in high glee. "I amused myself while we was in that Charleston hotel, amakin' up a lit twister I calc'lated might pan aout okay; an' she certain did me proud—took most two minutes fo' the spark to creep 'long an' touch things off. Whoopee! didn't them bimbos kick up a reg'lar jamboree though,

when the hull ship started in one big nest o' fire—
nawthin' like a nice sprinklin' o' gas to make things
hum."

"Shake hands again, Wally, boy—it takes a
cracker-jack like you to think up big things," and
Jack acted as though he took more genuine pleasure in having Perk make such a "bulls-eye" than
if he had occupied the spot-light himself.

They dropped into the cockpit of the old but re-
juvenated powerboat and were soon on their way
back to the secreted airship. Fortunately they ran
across nothing hostile while carefully following
the channel of the tortuous river; had another
speedboat laden with contraband come along back
of them they might have been hard put to hide,
since the oncoming craft would of necessity be using a searchlight, so as to buck the villainous current, as well as avoid snags, and half hidden rocks.

Jack was ready to give full credit to Jethro for
his wonderful success in locating every such ob-
stacle; once or twice they did happen to run softly
up against a submerged tree-trunk; but the pilot
had acute hearing, and sensed the fact that they
were approaching such a dangerous snag; for
he always reduced their speed, and the collision did
no harm whatever.

It took them double the time to get back to their
hiding-place as when going forth, all because of

that swift current; but in good order they finally arrived, somewhat weary, but feeling the uplifting ardor accompanying a perilous mission successfully carried out.

Now they meant to seek rest, and sleep. In the morning they would try and take things easy, having nothing to do while daylight lasted but eat, and doze, looking hopefully forward to making another such sally when darkness again covered the coast lands and waterways.

Perk must have been very contented with the fine showing he had made in their first assault on the enemy's lines of communication. He followed the example of his chum, lying down on one of the cots belonging to the cabin of the big amphibian —they had arranged blankets on the floor for Jethro, after he had positively refused to take one of the cots, saying he was "used tuh knockin' around, an' takin' pot-luck when he felt sleepy"— and just before passing into dreamland himself Jack heard his best pal mutter:

"Huh! fust blood fo' Uncle Sam's boys, which same is a good sign, I'd say!"

CHAPTER XXVII
The Luckless Speedboat

The night passed without anything in the nature of an alarm. Once when Jack chanced to wake up, he could catch the familiar pulsations of a cloud-chaser of an airship passing, at a considerable distance; and as near as he could figure, heading directly toward the rendezvous on the creek, where a descent would be made to the exact spot on which the other craft had so lately been mysteriously incinerated.

"I wonder if that turns out to be our next victim," was what the listener said under his breath, as he dropped back to continue his sleep.

In the morning it was deemed quite safe for Perk to build a cooking fire well back of the rise, so that even though a boat should pass up or down the river curious eyes would not be apt to see anything suspicious. The air, too, was favorable, since it came from a direction to leeward of the water, which would carry such light smoke as arose from the small fire safely away.

Perk gave himself and two companions a very acceptable breakfast, all things considered. He was possessed of a fair amount of culinary skill; dearly loved to get up a camp meal, and satisfy the yearnings of his always empty stomach; and moreover had selected a number of such viands as would appeal to the taste of three hungry men, reduced to their own cookery.

Afterwards Perk kept himself busy doing a number of things that had some connection with their comfort along the "grub line," as he termed it.

Jethro seemed content to just take things comfortably; while Jack found an abundance of employment in making up his notes. This was carried out in the code language, so that if he had the hard luck to fall into the hands of the enemy they would not be able to discover what all the queer marks really stood for—without a knowledge concerning the key it would seem more or less like the silly scribbling of a child.

Then, too, Jack allowed himself to figure out what would be the nature of their next undertaking, following out their plan for striking telling blows at everything that helped to build up the strategic working of the smuggler ring's illicit business.

"It should be tried out if another of those speedboats makes shore while we're hanging around up there," he told himself, after one of these spells of deep thinking; "anything that goes to create a feeling of genuine consternation in that mob comes along our line of action. We've prepared for all those kind of little surprises, and mustn't lose any chance that drifts our way, that's absolutely certain. Well, we'll wait and see what turns up to-night."

At noon Perk once again disappeared back of the screen of brush, vines and dense foliage, to concoct another fragrant and much relished meal. At night they would have to fare on cold stuff, as Jack hesitated to risk the glow of a fire so near the river, where some sort of boat might be passing, with a chance of discovery that would spell disaster to all their pet schemes.

As the afternoon moved along Jack cast uneasy glances up at the sky, where openings in the heavy belt of trees allowed of a fragmentary survey.

"Seems a little like rain, fellows," he told his mates; whereupon both of the others took a good look, and pronounced their several opinions.

Jethro, Jack found, proved to be one of those natural weather oracles such as may occasionally be run across among the natives in southern sections of the country; and his opinion struck both the others as sound and reasonable.

He even in his quaint fashion, and in the lingo of cracker land, explained on what he based his prophecy that, while the clouds might persist there would be no rain fall inside of twelve to twenty hours; although beyond that he was not prepared to say, and felt there was a fair chance the clouds would wet things pretty well before giving way to clear skies again.

"Mebbe then we kin put in one more good blast 'fore we git housed up here in aour houseboat," Perk advanced, as both his opinion and his secret wish.

"Let's hope so," Jack told him, to bolster up his already drooping spirits. "Anyhow, if it hasn't started to rain when we're ready to pull out tonight, it's agreed we'll not hold back on account of a little ducking."

"Yeou sed it, buddy," Perk snapped with avidity, accompanying the words with one of his old-time grins, that told of renewed expectation of fresh achievement.

So after they had partaken of some cold refreshment to stay their hunger, they completed their preparations for sallying forth to inflict further damage on the enemy, and add to their consternation by all possible measures.

Their course was identical with that pursued on the former occasion. It was darker than on the previous night, owing no doubt to the curtain of clouds that shut off even the friendly starlight. Jethro, however, proved to be equal to his task, and as they made but comparatively slow progress down the swift running stream managed to steer his boat without colliding with the obstacles lying in wait. These bobbed up now to the right, and again to the left—seething little whirlpools, and ugly pointed rocks, but partially out of water— just as in days of old in Grecian seas, mariners had to keep clear of Scylla and Charybdis, two monsters who threatened their craft with destruction, —the whirlpool on one hand, and a cruel-fanged monster rock on the other.

They eventually reached the spot for which they aimed, and again was the powerboat screened behind that accommodating natural curtain. Then, after a little delay while gathering certain things (the possession of which would save a tedious trip back to the boat, such as had been Perk's portion on that other occasion) the trio began their long crawl, with the idea of locating that inviting spot from whence they could view the camp, and yet be out of sight of the rough characters making up the working force of the smugglers.

To the dismay of Perk there was no airship awaiting action at the spot of the previous night's blaze. Evidently the one Jack had heard pass over —and of which he had informed both his comrades—must have passed out again to where the mother-ship lay at anchor; or else possibly sped back to some island like the depot at Bimini, where another cargo could be taken on.

"But they mebbe might slip in some time to-night," Perk told himself, in deadly fear that they were to have all their work for nothing, which would certainly have been too bad, and must grieve the honest fellow terribly.

As for Jack, he chanced to be thinking in quite a different direction.

It began to grow somewhat monotonous, just lying there and listening to what hilarious jokes and slangy conversation passed between the rough hired workers, smoking and drinking alongside the comfortable fires.

It was now getting along toward midnight, and they had been lying in that cramped condition for several hours. Some of the men had thrown themselves down near the fires, as though to pick up some sleep; but sagacious Jack noticed an air of expectation among them as a whole, which assured him they anticipated some fresh arrival, whether from the air or the river of course he could not say with certainty.

Presently he did notice that two of men who appeared to be leaders walked down to the crude wharf, and seemed to be changing things around as though preparing for coming shipments of contraband stuff.

"I figure it's going to be a boat," he told himself on seeing this movement—"they've had word of its coming, I reckon through that powerful radio station on the coast, which we're given orders to find, and knock out of business."

And a boat it proved to be, for shortly afterwards Jack caught a distant sound as of an engine working; and since it did not come from above it must be moving up the stream, having some time before entered at the mouth of the Yamasaw.

Before long they could detect the strong light that bore upstream, to show the pilot where to keep the nose of his craft. Later, the speedboat was tied to the dock by a capable hawser, and the labor of taking her heavy cargo ashore began.

Of course there was nothing that could be done to interfere with the landing of the contraband, and its being loaded on the waiting trucks. Their orders had been along different lines—they were to try and hurt the operations of the daring smuggler ring, kill it off if possible; but under no consideration risk the betrayal of their plan of campaign by trying to hinder some of the goods that were landed from reaching their far-away destinations as scheduled.

Jack, watching closely, soon saw the parties who manned the speedboat seemed in no particular hurry to start back down the river. Having delivered their valuable load of wet goods in security, they ran no risk of being seized by a revenue cutter, or contraband-chaser, if dawn should find them close off shore.

The two officers were sitting at a rough table chatting with several of the leading smugglers, and drinking something that looked like real champagne; while the balance of the crew had mingled with the campers, and seemed to be taking an hour or so off.

Jack having kept close tabs on all that went on felt confident there was not a single man aboard the speedboat. His hoped for opportunity was at hand, and no time must be lost.

So, having previously notified his mates what he meant to attempt, he now left them, carrying some small bundle along, the nature of which Perk understood very well since it was he himself who had hooked up the fire bomb with the time-clockwork that could be set for any minute necessary— and which was now arranged two hours ahead.
Jack soon found himself alongside the boat; and watching his chance he slipped aboard. He was not over five minutes at work, when he again appeared in the shadows alongside the rough wharf, from whence he readily made the shore.

When he a little afterwards rejoined his companions the order must have been given for the crew to get aboard, as the boat was scheduled to take off, perhaps to head for Charleston, or Georgetown, to pick up needed supplies that were regular, and not in the contraband class.

Those ashore gave their allies a round of cheers before the vessel vanished down the stream—why not when they surely had not anything to fear in the line of discovery? Those sneaking Secret Service agents had never bothered them seriously ever since the headquarters rendezvous was stationed at this hard to reach point on the twisting, turbulent Yamasaw.

"We'll hang out here for another hour and more," Jack whispered to his two backers. "I'm hoping to pick up some more valuable points from hearing the men chaffing one another—I'd give a lot just to know where that radio sending and receiving station is located, as it would save us considerable trouble in combing the entire coast of South Carolina."

"Yeah," Perk was saying, oh! so softly—no one hearing his customary manner of speech would ever imagine he could modulate his voice so wonderfully—"an' I shore reckons we kin see the fine light that's laid aout for Fo'th o' July celebration on this late Fall night, jest as good up hyah as daown thar."

"A heap better, Wally," Jack assured him.

The time passed tediously to active Perk. He had listened eagerly as long as the sound of the working engines of the elegant speedboat could be heard down the river; but by degrees they grew fainter, until even keen-eared Perk was unable to place them.

Long afterwards he drew the attention of his mates to what seemed a queer illumination up in the clouded heavens toward the southeast.

"Huh! kinder seems like sumpin' might be agoin' on over yonder, suh," was what he said in Jack's ears; "which I has a most pow'ful notion has to do with aour purty racin' boat what's more'n likely kicked her heels at many a rev'nue cutter that couldn't close in on her nohaow."

"You said it that time, Wally," Jack assured him, feeling a little thrill himself over the probable success of his attempt at wiping out yet another of those swift air and water vehicles engaged in doing the transportation for the wholesale smugglers' combination.

Some of those in the camp had by this time also taken note of the tell-tale crimson stain on the low-hanging clouds, for they began to watch it in considerable surprise, as well as uneasiness. What had happened on the preceding night was only too fresh in their minds for them to forget the unaccountable nature of the disaster.

"Gosh! we shore got 'em guessin', partner," Perk was saying, softly, after they were once more aboard the old and faithful powerboat, with cat-eyed Jethro at the steering wheel, guiding the boat's destinies by sheer intuition and good hearing combined.

"Looks that way, brother," was the other's terse but eloquent reply.

They met with no accident while on their way back to their "location," as Perk sometimes referred to the hidden camp, he having been out with companies of Hollywood people when making pictures demanding rural surroundings, and consequently picking up a few of their customary designations.

They had just managed to get safely aboard the amphibian when the first rain-drop came down; and in less than ten minutes it was pouring; evidently Nature herself was in league with Jack and his allies to favor their undertakings in a friendly as well as most admirable fashion.

CHAPTER XXVIII
Ready for Another Blow

That rain put a damper on their plans, all right, for it kept up intermittently for many hours. To be sure, they were comfortable enough, housed in the cabin of the big amphibian, and with plenty of good "eats" at hand, as well as soft drinks in abundance—what a grand forager that same Perk would make if the occasion should ever arrive where it was necessary to "live off the country," as many an invading army has found itself compelled to do.

At least neither of his companions had any cause to "knock" the said Perk for the least dereliction along the line of supplies—backed by abundant resources in the way of funds, supplied by a generous Republic, he always found it a pleasure to lay in stock—and help make way with the same in addition, it must be confessed.

When night came there was no clear spot in all the heavens—only a vast gray curtain shrouding everything in gloom. And through the night at regular intervals fresh showers arrived to further moisten things.

Jack knew there would be nothing doing on the following night, since, even if the persistent clouds did choose to disperse, the ground and bushes would be much too well saturated for them to think of crawling on hands or knees, or "snaking" it along on their stomachs, so close to the hostile camp—they must exercise their patience, and await yet another twenty-four hours.

This long stretch of idleness was especially hard on poor Perk. From the day of his birth he had always been a "doer," and no shirk; so that when compelled to just "loaf around sucking his thumbs," as he so eloquently described the situation, he felt absolutely dejected.

Indeed, there were times when Jack had to almost use force in the effort to compel his near pal to "hold his horses," and wait for the sky to clear up. Perk grumbled, and incessantly poked his head out of the cabin to ascertain if the expected break was yet in sight.

So another night gathered its shades about them; but they had seen the sun go down amidst a generous flush, which welcome sign of fair weather in the offing was accepted as most promising.

"Hot-diggetty-dig!" Perk was heard to say time and time again, as he prepared the evening meal; from which service he seemed to extract a meed of comfort; "mebbe naow I aint joyful over the chanct to be doin' somethin' once more. Never could keep my head straight when things they kept agoin' ev'ry which way fo' Sunday. An' I'm shore all a twist to help knock yet another ship silly—the more the merrier sez I—we gotter to pound it inter the nobs o' them ducks they caint meddle with a buzz saw owned by Unc. Sam, an' git away with hit. Ev'rybody pull up to the table—soup's on."

Which it was for a fact, since he had heated up a tin of excellent vegetable concoction that helped warm them up—the continual rain having chilled the air, and made things "shivery," as Perk kept saying disconsolately enough.

It was a long night to every one in the little company.

They had dozed so often during the last two days, that nobody felt very much like turning in; and at that slept fitfully; so that never was a dawn welcomed more heartily than daylight on the next morning.

The sun soon brought a fresh cheer with it, and as there was not a single cloud in the blue skies it looked as though by evening things would have dried up in a way to please the entire trio, with an opportunity for work at hand.

Again did Perk go over the list of things they would necessarily take along, not intending there should arise any hitch in the plan through want of forethought on his part.

The start was made in complete darkness.

Jack found himself hoping that their luck might stay by them for another spell; and that Jethro, who up to that hour had done so exceptionally well, might be able to keep up the good work.

It was bound to be a bit more difficult reaching their former hiding place, for several good reasons, Jack figured. In the first place the gloom that wrapped such a cloak about them would cause their guide additional trouble, in order to avoid coming into rough collision with one of those ambushing snags, or half concealed rocks.

Then again by this time they might expect the suspicions of their enemies must have been more or less awakened, making them more watchful, also restless.

Probably those at the camp rendezvous may have before then been informed concerning the mysterious burning of the speedboat carrier of contraband stuff, while on the way down the Yamasaw heading for the sea. That significant fact, coupled with the destruction of the airship within hand-throw of their campfires, would surely begin to awaken certain fears to the extent that some strange series of disasters had overtaken the long run of luck they had been enjoying in landing all their precious cargoes without a single break.

Jack noticed how their cracker guide kept on his way at a slower speed, and he found himself mentally commending this degree of caution. Evidently Jethro too, was bent on making certain nothing in the line of an upset to their game could be laid at his door.

Just after they started the sound of a motor was clearly heard, and somehow every head was immediately lifted toward the heavens; for there could not be any difficulty in realizing the racket came from that quarter, making it clear an airship was passing by.

"There she blows, mates!" Perk breathed, exultantly. "Things air aworkin' agin in aour favor, seems like. Go it, ole boy; we got yeour number, and kin fix yeou aout right smart."

"Lower your voice if you must speak, Wally," cautioned Jack, apprehensively, since there was no knowing what the darkness concealed from their eyes.

"But she's amakin' fo' that same camp, I kinder gu—reckon—aint she, Boss?" continued the irrepressible Perk.

"To be sure," Jack told him; "and now please dry up, brother."

The clatter died away, from which they fancied the incoming ship must have made a successful landing. In imagination Perk could vision what was taking place—the eager workers picking up whatever the pilots of the air carrier tossed out of their spacious cabin, and possibly loading the same on some waiting truck, or at least a speedy automobile, functioned by a capable chauffeur, who had interest in the stake.

Onward they continued, and all kept going well, from which fact Jack figured that thus far the smugglers had not deemed it essential to have videttes posted along the river, in order to keep tabs on what might be going on.

To himself Jack was deciding that, should they be fortunate enough to make way with yet another cargo carrier on this present night, he would feel it judicious to change his base of attack, and go after that mysterious radio sending station, without which the plans of the lawless crowd would be just about "knocked on the head."

"They must be depending absolutely on the information that passes between the mother ship and the shore, to shape all these successful landings," was the way he mentally put it; "and once we put the kibosh on that secret radio shop their hands will be tied; so that the regular force of Coast Guards, backed by the fast revenue cutters, and speedboats taken over by the Government, will be able to keep things down at a low ebb."

Much depended on whether they would be able to accomplish a third stroke, so as to complete the perplexity, and awaken the concern of the smugglers. Jack felt tolerably certain that once they had aroused a lively feeling bordering on *fear* among those rough men, they would be apt to magnify things, and fancy that the long arm of the Law was reaching out with irresistible power, to clutch them with remorseless tenacity, and start them on the road to the penitentiary at Atlanta.

That was his present goal—if only he might institute a reign of apprehension among them the end would be in sight—from the beginning this had taken its place in his mind as the main object of his crusade; and so it meant a great deal for them to hit again at the enemy without any further delay.

Arriving at the place where the powerboat was to be secreted they soon found themselves making for the vicinity of the camp, the fires of which served them as a target, such as pilots on a crooked Florida river use in order to avoid pitfalls in the shape of snags along their course.

When they were once more installed in their customary shelter Perk saw with a feeling of vast relief that sure enough another plane was in sight.

CHAPTER XXIX

Jethro Takes a Hand

"Lookey, Jack, it's a crate 'bout like ourn—an amphibian, an' a beaut in the bargain. What great luck, oh boy!" was what Perk was whispering into his chum's ear.

"I see it—let up on the talk,—we've got to plan quick, for fear the ship takes off again!" Jack told him, vexed because his pal seemed unable to bridle his tongue when silence was what they most needed.

He could see the two men who had come with the amphibian, since they were still wearing their service togs, and helmets. They seemed to be enjoying themselves hugely with some of the occupants of the main camp; as though in a high humor because of their successful flight, and safe arrival.

"What kinder ship be that, partner?" demanded the one who could not be effectually squelched.

"I don't know—looks mighty like one of those new multi-motored Kingbirds, with a big cabin that might hold a dozen passengers. Now please hold your breath, Wally, and let me *think*—we've got to work fast for they'll take off any time now."

Jack having already about decided on their line of action was not long in reaching a conclusion. It was to be the turn of Jethro now—he had promised the other he should have his inning, under the conviction that the guide had earned a right to strike one good blow, so as to feel he had thus avenged his family wrongs at the hands of John Haddock.

A hurried consultation in whispers followed. Then Jethro backed away, with some object carefully tucked under an arm. When he was beyond the range of their limited observation Jack touched Perk on the arm.

"We're moving our base, brother," he told him most cautiously. "Jethro has only a regular bomb to set, and will have to scuttle out of that in something of a hurry. They may start a search, and come this way; so we ought to be on our way to the boat."

"Shucks! naow aint that jest too bad—yeou're abreakin' my heart, Boss—I shore did want to see that ship smashed to flinders," whispered the chagrined Perk.

"We may yet—I know of another place further back, where it'd be safe for us to stop, and then hurry off after it happens."

In this fashion then did Jack smother the budding mutiny on Perk's part; so they began their retrograde movement, with all their senses on the alert to avoid any hovering danger.

From all the indications Jack had already guessed the smugglers were on nettles and pins concerning the meaning of the late disasters that had struck their hitherto smooth running machine— they had been turning their heads this way and that, as if uneasy, casting frequent anxious glances toward the big and costly airship (that undoubtedly had only lately become a regular visitor at the rendezvous camp), as if tempted to believe it too might suddenly burst into flames, as though some mysterious and powerful electrical ray were at work, bringing destruction in its wake.

Arriving at the back refuge mentioned by observing Jack, they crouched down and waited for whatever was fated to come to pass. Jack himself felt a bit anxious, wondering whether it had been a wise thing to allow inexperienced Jethro to handle this last hazard—what if he managed to make a mess of it in spite of his good intentions, and all the teaching he, Jack, had given him? On the other hand there was always a possibility that some restless member of the gang suddenly decide to step over, and see if everything was well with the expensive addition to their air force—should such an investigator run smack up against their cracker guide in the act of setting his bomb, the result might be a premature explosion that would prove disasterous to poor Jethro, even though it also destroyed the expensive ship.

Perk was holding his breath with eagerness, only taking an occasional gulph when it became absolutely necessary. Jack, too, admitted to feeling his usually well trained nerves tingling with mingled sensations as the minutes crept on and nothing came to pass.

Then suddenly without the slightest warning it happened—there was a most dazzling illumination, very like a nearby flash of lightning, and accompanied by a frightful explosion that actually almost caused the two watchers to fall flat on their backs.

They had a glimpse however, of a vast upheaval, as the new amphibian was cast up skyward in fragments, even the weighty motors being hurled aloft, to speedily come back to earth with dreadful force. Every man in the camp had been blown off his feet, and could be seen toppling in all directions.

Jack clutched Perk by the arm, and gave him a tug which the other understood meant they must cut for the boat with another instant's delay. The last thing they glimpsed was the various prostrate figures scrambling to their feet, and naturally hurrying forward, risking being injured by the still falling fragments of what had so recently been a beautiful sample of the very latest up-to-date cabin tri-motored passenger airship, sponsored, if Jack had guessed rightly, by one of the foremost building corporations known to the world of aviation.

They managed to arrive in safety at their goal, and to Jack's great relief found faithful Jethro awaiting their coming, full to the brim with joy over the consummation of his scheme for revenge long since over-due.

The clamor from the camp was still at high ebb, men shouting all manner of exciting things, as they endeavored to recover their wits enough to try and figure out what it could all mean.

Once upon the river and the fugitives began to make some sort of speed. No longer did they feel any necessity for using caution, save to avoid the traps formed by those persistent snags, and other obstructions to a safe passage. No one could overtake them, thanks to the speed of the old reconstructed powerboat, as well as the skill of its pilot; and once they reached the hidingplace of their amphibian how easy for them to take to the air, leaving Jethro's boat where the plane had been hidden?

Then for the grand climax to their adventure—finding the secret radio station, and sending it in the wake of the destroyed speedboat, also the two smuggler airships that would no longer carry contraband loads across land and water from near-by foreign islands, or mother ships anchored off the east coast.

CHAPTER XXX

The Wind-up—Conclusion

They found it easy enough to get up speed with the assistance of the current, and then take off, when a clear streak of water was reached. Rising to a fair ceiling Jack headed south, and the night flight was on.

He let Perk take over the controls before a great while, while once again he studied his charts, well marked from previous searchings. So went the long hours, with numerous turnings as the humor urged; for they were now only killing time, and waiting for the dawn to come.

No sooner was it light than Jack again settled down at the stick, with the ship headed toward his intended goal. He had good reason to believe his information to be correct, and that before many hours they would be able to cash in on the prospect, kill the efficiency of the outlaw radio station to do further injury, and bring the operations of the great smuggler league to a wind-up, which was all the Government asked of him.

Nine o'clock in the morning found them on the coast, and approaching a certain wild district where no man was supposed to have his habitation—even the shanties of the Spring fishermen were conspicious by their absence—the place was so lonely, so isolated, so storm-swept, that the bravest of coast dwellers did not have the nerve to carry on their daily avocation along the line of fishing, or wild-fowl shooting, amidst such desolate surroundings.

All of which had made it an ideal spot for an unregistered radio base; and Jack believed his hunch was a true one when he decided he would find the end of his trail where he was now heading.

A little distance back of the beach, beyond the scrub and dead grass, there had for many years been known to exist a strange looking object, almost falling in ruins now; but which at one time had been a well built tower, more or less fashioned after the type of a coast lighthouse, since it had winding stairs within, and a room at the top, from which a wonderful view of the sea could be obtained.

Jack knew the brief history of that queer tower —how it had been built long years back by a retired sea captain, whose heart was still faithful to his beloved salt-water; and who, desirous of dying within the sound of the breakers had spent almost his last dollar in having this peculiar tower erected, strong enough with its rocky walls to defy the elements that usually played such rough pranks along this particular stretch of shore.

Some people of a romantic turn of mind even said the old captain had lost his wife and daughter in a wreck close by that very part of the coast, which fact had been mainly instrumental in his carrying out his queer conceit. After all, he had really died there, being found lifeless by a party of shipwrecked men who chanced to reach land at that place, and anticipated being fed and warmed by some genial light keeper, only to discover but a dead man there. A nephew had seen to his burial, stripped the "observatory" of everything of value, and forsook all else. Now the tower was a near-ruin, and in danger of toppling when some unusually severe gale swept the water over the sand ridge, and against the "castle" wall.

When Perk glimpsed the object of their solicitude far away Jack brought his ship down on the beach, and taxied back to where he had reason to believe it would be safe from the highest tide.

Then they set out to stalk their intended prey, keeping far enough back so as to avoid being detected by any trained eyes from the room in the top of the dead sea captain's lone tower.

By noon they had gained enough distance to be able to keep watch on the tower through means of Perk's glasses. They soon discovered signs of life about the place, which fact gratified them greatly; surely no rational human being would ever take up his abode in that ramshackle affair unless he had some unusually important reason for so doing, such was its inaccessibility, and lonesome condition, there being not even duck shooting available, while the fishing must be equally *non est*.

By one o'clock they were able to figure that there were just two men in the tower, which reckoning allowed the formation of a concrete plan of action.

It appeared that just one of these fellows was on duty at a time, the other apparently being free to wander off, if the notion struck him. Possibly, too, most of their work came along after night had set in, since business picked up at that hour.

"The next time either one steps out to take a little saunter I'll follow in a roundabout way, and nab him when he isn't dreaming of danger. After I've stopped him from giving the alarm, and putting his mate on guard I'll give a signal for you lads to swing around and approach the junk-shop by keeping hidden behind that sand hill. Once I get my foot on the steps leading up inside the tower it'll be all over but the shouting. Soak that in, both of you boys?"

Which they said they would; and so Jack a little later on, crept off, exercising great care as he picked up his duty to keep hidden from those lookout windows at the summit of the said tower.

He managed to take up a position where it was most likely the walker would pass close by, and there he stood, sheltered from view. The chap was amazingly stunned to have something thrust him in the back, and to hear a stern voice say:

"Not a single word or you're a dead man! We've got the tower surrounded, even if you don't see my men; and the game is played out. You're under arrest for sending out illegal radio calls that are in the interest of coast smugglers and other criminal parties. Silence now, or I'll crack you over the head."

It was almost what Perk would call a "picnic," things fell into their hands so easily. Having bound and gagged his prisoner Jack made his way back to a point close to the leaning tower, when he gave the promised signal; and was speedily joined by his two mates.

After that they all three went cautiously up the winding stairs, and suddenly took the remaining radio man by surprise, by covering him with three guns, and cowing him in the bargain. Realizing that the game was queered he did not dare take desperate chances by putting up any resistance; simply grinning, and holding out his hands for Jack to slip the bracelets over his wrists.

"Now," explained Jack, "the only thing we want

to do is to take some of this stuff along to prove we've demolished the offending radio-sending station; after which it's up to Uncle Sam to see that this scotched snake doesn't show its head again along the same lines—we will have finished our job in first-class shape, and can take up something else, for to be sure there's work aplenty for us Secret Service lads."

Before this was carried out Jack secured a fine picture of the old leaning Coast Tower, as well as its interior, showing the radio sending outfit just as they found it. This being accomplished as positive evidence that could not be successfully disputed, they put aside such material as could be readily transported in the cabin of their amphibian, and then sent the racketty tower high up in the air, to fall in fragments on the beach.

After that all of them boarded the ship, and they set out for Charleston, to drop Jethro—who would sooner or later hear from the two chums, as well as receive a fat reward for the part he had taken in rounding up the smuggler gang, and putting that mischievous radio out of the running—also turning over the two prisoners to the care of Mr. Herriott, as representative of the legal branch of the Government. What became of them Jack and Perk neither knew nor cared, as other equally thrilling happenings soon came along to occupy their time and attention, to the exclusion of matters that were now "has-beens," hull down in the past.

They first of all turned over that admirable amphibian, the remodeled Curtiss cabin twin-motored ship, to the authorities; and when they left Charleston it was aboard their own familiar plane, the big Fokker. In some succeeding volume it may be taken for granted we shall again meet those two interesting aerial Soldiers of Fortune, Jack Ralston and Perk, doing their perilous stunts in some other field of adventure, the narration of whose exploits may form the basis of the next book in this *Sky Detective Series.*

THE END.